OASIS

◄◄•►►

BY GREGORY MAGUIRE

Clarion Books/New York

Clarion Books
a Houghton Mifflin Company imprint
215 Park Avenue South, New York, NY 10003
Text copyright © 1996 by Gregory Maguire

Type is set in 12/14.5 point Garamond

For information about this and other Houghton Mifflin trade and reference books and multimedia products, visit The Bookstore at Houghton Mifflin on the World Wide Web at (http://www.hmco.com/trade/).

Printed in the U.S.A.

Library of Congress Cataloging-in-Publication Data
Maguire, Gregory.
Oasis / by Gregory Maguire.
p.   cm.
Summary: Following his father's death from a heart attack, thirteen-year-old Hand blames himself and his mother, who has recently returned after leaving the family years ago.
ISBN 0-395-67019-5
[1. Death—Fiction.   2. Mothers and sons—Fiction.]   I. Title.
PZ7.M2762Oas   1995
[Fic]—dc20   94-42891
                                                  CIP
                                                  AC

BP   10   9   8   7   6   5   4   3   2   1

This book is for Rafique Keshavjee—
at long last, and with love

CONTENTS

Part One

The Bustle in a House
The Morning after Death
Is solemnest of industries
Enacted upon Earth—

The Sweeping up the Heart
And putting Love away
We shall not want to use again
Until Eternity.

⊷ one ⊶

Hand Gunther found his dad's body early on an evening in May. It was slumped on the floor of the canteen, rolled across a doormat that said WELCOME. From the radio, Lite Rock was bubbling away, all the hits all the time. Outside, birds were noisily happy.

Hand knew this was death, though he couldn't have said how, since he'd never seen it before. He slid over the threshold of the canteen and lifted his dad up, remembered from movies that you should loosen a collar, slap color into the cheeks, feel at the wrist or the neck for a pulse. The sweat on his dad's face was awful, like the cold moisture on a bologna. And then he dropped him, gently, because he was too heavy, and said, "Sorry Daddy, sorry," as if his dad could hear.

Unless his father wasn't really dead. Hand lunged toward the office. The motel they'd bought this past winter was pretty empty this week, no lodgers around to help. So Hand would have to make the frantic call to 911 himself. He could see it:

3

the ambulance, the emergency maneuvers, the brutal smacking of someone back to life, with those hand-held power jolters like steam irons. But even as he ran, weeping and gulping without feeling it, Hand knew it was too late. His dad was gone.

"Atonquit Falls police and fire," said a voice with good humor in it. "This is Shirley. . . . Hello there? . . . Are you there?"

"Please"—Hand's voice worked at last—"please, my father's fallen, send an ambulance—"

Shirley went all businesslike. "Location . . . Name of patient . . . Your name . . . Are you alone, dear?"

Hand stood motionless at the telephone, couldn't speak to that. He wasn't alone, because his dad was there; he was alone though, because his dad *wasn't* there.

"Look," Shirley was saying, "look honey, you go outside and wait for the fellows. Sit on the doorstep and look for them. I'll dispatch them right away. It'll be all right, honey. Don't go back in—if he's still conscious he'll just be upset that *you're* upset. Got that? Hang on, honey, won't be but a mo." Before she had even hung up, he could hear Shirley bawling into an intercom, "Fred, a Code Blue at the Oasis Motel on Route Twelve—that's the dump about a mile beyond the Sunoco station—" Hand did as he was told, as if he were a small child. Each car that came out of Atonquit Falls was full of family: fathers going home from

4

work, mothers with kids. There wasn't an ambulance for a million years. While he waited, the dog from across the way came to sniff the dumpster, as it did every evening.

Hand could hear the weather report following the six-o'clock radio news. "What a day it was in Berkshire County today!" said the deejay jubilantly. "High seventies and low humidity, and no black flies yet: a day to remember!"

◄◄-►►

Hand didn't watch their labors over his father. He couldn't, and they wouldn't have let him even if he had wanted to. They strapped Rudy Gunther onto a stretcher and wheeled him into the ambulance. The driver was a big fat guy with two tattoos saying *Janice* and *Give @!%&! Peace a Chance!* "Where's your mother?" he asked Hand.

"She doesn't live here."

"Well, where? Come on, get in the front, Fred'll ride in the back with your pa. Where's your mom, pal?"

"On the West Coast, in Seattle."

"You know her phone number? We'll have to call her."

They didn't talk until they got to the Atonquit Falls/Buxton Medical Center, a squat building with white aluminum siding and black aluminum shutters, and a nurse watering the flowers. She dropped the hose and ran to help Fred and the

5

tattooed, beer-bellied guy haul his father out. They raced the stretcher through several sets of swinging doors. Hand wasn't allowed to follow through the last set.

The nurse came back quickly. She fussed with her eyeglasses and studied a clipboard.

"Tell me, is it bad?" said Hand. He began to hope he'd overreacted—just the normal panic at the idea of being abandoned.

"Look," she said, "there's like this form we have to do. Who's the next of— Who're your relatives? Mom away on business—anyone else?"

"Mom's *not* away on business. She lives there. She left Daddy when I was ten."

The nurse got very professional. She read back the information to make sure it was right:

Patient's name: Rudolf Gunther.

Occupation: teacher at Atherton Academy, and also owner and manager, Oasis Motel, Atonquit Falls, Massachusetts.

Age: 41.

Marital status: separated.

Wife: Clare Foxworthy Gunther. Lives in Seattle.

Daughter: Davida Gunther, 19, freshman at Bennington College.

Son: Mohandas Gunther, resides with father, Atonquit Falls. Age 13. Atherton Academy Middle School.

"Any aunts or uncles in Atonquit Falls?" The nurse peered at him over the top of her glasses. "Any cousins? Family friends?"

"We just moved here in December," said Hand. "We used to live in Radley. We haven't gotten to know anyone yet."

"Who's your best friend at school then?" Hand shrugged at that. The new school wasn't being so terrific.

The nurse offered him a mint. He sucked on it with long sighs, intaking air moistly around his side teeth. She went away. Another nurse came by with a damp mess of coffee grounds in a soggy filter, saying to no one in particular, "They should pay the evening shift extra for housekeeping." Pretty soon the first nurse came back, with a woman in a blue plaid shirt who said she was Dr. Cavanaugh.

The doctor sat down as an old comfortable friend might do, leaned forward, and took his hands in her own. "Hand," she said, "your father died sometime this afternoon. Probably very quickly. I've put in a call to the principal of your school. He's on his way here."

Hand just sat there, numb.

◄◄•►►

Mr. Brown, the principal of Atherton Academy, knew Hand's father well. Rudy Gunther used to teach in a school in Rhode Island, and Mr. Brown had been the principal there, too. Mr. Brown was an older man who sounded as if he were English, though he was born and raised in Philadelphia.

People called him Old Money. He was kindly, he moved slowly, as if his bones might splinter, and he was boring.

He got Hand settled into a guest bedroom, all aggressively clean with the smell of Lemon Pledge and pressed pillowcases. Copies of *Atherton Academy Today* were arranged in a display fan on the windowseat. "Pull yourself together, young Hand. We'll call your mother for you," he said. "Letitia is a wonder at times like this." Letitia was Mr. Brown's wife, a puckered, lavendery lady who gave teas for the boys and painted modern pictures with shocking nakedness in them, if you looked hard enough.

Hand went into the bathroom because it was a private bathroom, connected with the room, just like in the motel. It had a glass dish with red soap the color of fireballs in it. He locked the door and sat down on the lid of the toilet, thinking about the afternoon at school.

His father must have died while Hand was at track practice. Taking his time showering and dressing. Horsing around with the guys afterward, or trying to. Trying to pretend he was one of them. There was that mildewy damp smell of showers, and the rot of well-used sneakers, and the bare light bulbs in their cages making glossy reflections on wet skin. The ring of voices against metal lockers, the swearing and sex jokes, the clean pair of underpants tossed in the john, someone pretending his sock was a condom. Boy stuff.

He should've called to say he'd be late. That was the household rule. But he hadn't, and now his dad was dead.

His dad hadn't been in the office, which was strange. Still Hand hadn't given it a second thought. He went into the kitchen expecting there'd be a pot of SpaghettiOs gently burning on the stove. None of the four regular lodgers were around. It was only when Hand realized he was getting hungry that he started to wander around, looking for his dad. First he went to the mailbox, picking up the usual sheaf of catalogues and junk mail and bills, and then he headed over to the canteen. If Dr. Cavanaugh was right, his dad was already dead by then. Suppose Hand had skipped track practice? Suppose he had called home as he was supposed to do? Would his father be alive now?

There was a rap on the bathroom door; Hand jumped, as if he'd been caught doing something he shouldn't. "Be right out," he called. He ran the sink water for a minute, then opened the door.

Mr. Brown said, "Well, Hand, Letitia has your mother on the line now, and she's filling her in on the sorry news. I should guess you'd want to say something to her."

"No," said Hand.

Mr. Brown looked sad. "Are you sure?" he asked.

"I don't want to, if you don't mind," said Hand, "but I'll talk to my sister, Vida. Vida is sort of emotional."

"Well, I'll give you a holler as soon as we reach

9

your sister." Mr. Brown lumbered away down the hall. Letitia's flutey voice came up between the banisters of the half-circle staircase. At the top step Mr. Brown turned back and raised his eyebrows. "It would be a kindness to talk to your mother," he said gently.

"NO," said Hand.

◄◄-►►

Hand slept poorly. He kept hoping, in the foggy depths of his dreams, that the door would open and someone would come in. In the morning, he guessed maybe he had been waiting for Mr. Brown to tell him that Vida had been reached. But this didn't happen until just before breakfast. Vida was hysterical on the phone, crying and cursing one minute and full of organization the next. She was a comfort, in a strange sort of way: She seemed to be capable of the correct kind of public grief. Her howling was irritating and soothing at once.

Over a breakfast Hand had no appetite for, he listened to Mr. and Mrs. Brown arrange his day. "Flights from the West Coast arrive in mid-afternoon," said Mr. Brown, "but I'm not sure which flight, so there's no point going to the airport. Hand's mother will fly into Albany or Bradley International, whichever one she can get a flight to. She said she'll rent a car and call us from the Oasis when she gets there. One of us can bring Hand over then."

"Why can't my mother come here?" said Hand.

"Well, your mother doesn't know exactly when she'll arrive. She said she thinks it best if she meets you on your own home ground. She knows it's been a long time, Hand. What is it, two years?"

"Three, but who's counting?" said Hand. "Anyway, I want to be there when she gets there. It's more my home than hers. She never even saw it before. I can walk over this afternoon and wait by myself, thanks."

"Oh, you shouldn't have to do that," said Mrs. Brown kindly. "I'll come with you."

"I'm always there alone—I'm used to it."

"It's up to you," said Mr. Brown.

"Prentiss, the boy is only thirteen," said Mrs. Brown.

"It's been a long time since he's seen his mother, and we shouldn't interfere unless he wants us there," said Mr. Brown sharply.

"It's okay, really," said Hand. "I know what she *looks* like."

But in fact he wasn't sure. He was glad he didn't have to meet her airplane, as he'd probably say, "Hi there, Mom," to some total stranger.

"I don't approve," said Mrs. Brown frostily, but gave up the battle.

◄◄•►►

Hand was watching from his room, a little tent-shaped space fitted over the office and under the

11

roof. It had three low windows befurred with cobwebs and old bug carcasses. Through the flyspecks he saw his mother for the first time since he was ten. She arrived alone in a rented car. In a snappy, red-flowered suit that made her look younger than he remembered.

Ready, as ready as he could be. Three years of turning down her invitations to come live with her. Three years of confusion: anger sometimes, guilt at other times, and always regret. The kind mother of his young childhood had turned into the monster mother of his early teens. He knew he had to try to be fair to her, but he was afraid he would hate her, and it would show. Or that he would love her, and it *wouldn't* show. And even more afraid that he wouldn't be able to sort it out, figure it out.

By the time he got downstairs, she was in the office, glancing through the register. Making herself at home. "Hi, Mom," he said.

"Hand," she said, "hand to Hand," an old baby joke, a clapping game played by mother and son, "Hand to heart," she said, a suspicious quaver in there, stagey. "My boy—my teenager!"

She went in for a bear hug, as if it had been a couple of weeks instead of three years. She rubbed his head and murmured something, a sort of throaty hum he couldn't interpret. He held his mother loosely, as if she were a skeleton, but pulled back as soon as he felt he could. She paid no attention to his awkwardness, and she moved on to police reports and Vida's bus schedule and the funeral arrangements.

"How are you, Mom?" he said, hanging around. Well, he felt he had so little training on how to be with a mother; he wasn't sure what was okay and what was dorky.

"Rough and ready. Clinging on." She turned her head away. "And you?"

"You look great."

"I look like your mother," she said, sounding almost disgusted. Then she laughed. "I'm not complaining. *You* look so handsome, Hand! Growing shoulders! And that hair's gone platinum! I should be so pretty."

There was nothing to say to that. Hand wandered off to get a glass of iced tea, a kind of time-out in this forced reunion. And then he tried to pay attention to the details of the occasion.

"Hand, pick out a tie to bury Daddy in."

"Mom, Daddy never wore ties."

"Pick one out anyway."

"Why?"

"Oh, you're a teenager, I forget, arguing is like breathing. Never mind, I'll do it myself."

A few minutes later, another round.

"Hand, are we going to let Daddy's dizzy radical friends take over the funeral service?"

"I don't care, Mom."

"Well I've sure forfeited *my* right to an opinion, so it's up to you and Vida."

"I don't *care* what happens, Mom."

13

"Of course you care," she said, annoyed. "It's your father we're talking about, Hand. Don't tell me you don't care. You're just moping around to punish yourself." She was unpacking her suitcase and putting her clothes in his father's dresser, in his father's closet, as if she were just returning from a business trip. "Or to punish me. Well, just get over it and be some help, will you?"

"Would you like me to put your suitcase in the storeroom," he said, in extreme and oily helpfulness, "or should I leave it open on this chair so it's more convenient for you to pack up as soon as the funeral's over?"

⊷ two ⊷

Hand was standing in the cloakroom of Irish's. He had just made it past a clot of mourners signing themselves into the guest book. His head swam and his armpits itched. The air-conditioning unit, hidden behind a door under the stairs, rattled as if some nuts and bolts needed tightening.

His father was in the parlor, a stiff in a business suit, in the mahogany box with the ivory taffeta pillow and the puckered upholstery lining. Looking like wax. His mother was standing at the end of the coffin but was turned away from it. Hand hadn't seen her glance at the body once. She grabbed hands and kissed the air next to people's faces.

"Vida, where's your brother?" he heard her say. "I'd like him to meet someone."

He shrank back, almost impaling himself on a coathook.

Vida periscoped around but didn't see him. Tall, she could look over scalps and perms, but she'd been busy blowing her nose and keeping her outlandish black lace mantilla out of the way.

Hand couldn't stand to meet one more old friend of Rudy Guther's. His father must have had a thousand acquaintances now putting themselves forward as intimate pals. Folks were oozing trickles of tears in every corner of the place. Limp wasted handkerchiefs, varnished eyes, hands twisting into each other with nervous energy and feeling.

Except in the cloakroom, where Hand stood alone, his fists opening and closing.

"Vida," came his mother's voice, "would you find your brother, please? I need him to meet—"

He didn't catch the name. Without thinking about it, he opened the half-size door to the space under the stairs and flung himself inside, almost hugging the air conditioner. He was surprised he could fit; even though Vida was six years older, he was already taller than she was.

He couldn't figure out why they called it a funeral *home*. Thick-piled, silencing carpet. A wallpaper of ghostly green ferns. Rampant flowers, a hothouse gone berserk. And the cheesy, chummy nudge of recorded organ music playing tunes you keep almost recognizing.

"Hand?" Vida's voice called from just outside the door. "You around?"

She *had* seen him.

"I won't turn you in," she said in a low but carrying tone. To their mother, she meant. She kicked the door lightly with a Gucci toe. "You in there?"

He sighed noisily, not knowing whether he wanted her to hear or not. She went away.

Hand considered himself an ordinary joe. B average in school, when he tried. Not a jock, though he was on the track team. Not a brain, though he liked movies and comic books. He'd been a good son to his father, he thought; not a pushover, but not a troublemaker either. He balanced like a little kid who has to play alone on the seesaw. The only place to play is in the middle, one foot on either side, moving the seats up and down by yourself. The *plus* of this was control. The *minus* was the absence of risk or the chance of a better view.

Everything in his life had trained him to be prepared. But this, his father in there: This was beyond anything he'd expected to have to balance his way through.

Part of it was just the look of things. The morticians must have pinked up his father's cheeks with rouge. Or maybe it was the reflection on his skin of so many roses. His father's face had never been ruddy; it had been pale and open. Dead, his face had shut, like a snail retreating into its shell.

"So where's Hand?" A male voice he didn't recognize.

"Oh, he's around." Vida sounded intense and intimate with the someone. "He'll turn up."

"He must be so upset."

"He doesn't show it," said Vida. "Unlike Daddy, who used to cry at New England Telephone commercials."

"Stiff upper lip, like Clare." The voice was guarded—someone who knew their mother.

"Yes," said Vida dryly. "She's stiff, all right." There was a silence, then light flooded the compartment as the door was wrenched open and Vida's face burst into the dark. "Hand, you *are* in there. Come on out. Uncle Max and Uncle Emil are here, and the aunts, and Uncle Wolfgang, who has been looking for you. And who *else* just arrived but Grandma and Grandpa Foxworthy. The place is shaping up for a major skirmish. Come on, you and I are the U.N. peacekeeping force."

"Leave me alone."

"I need your help," said Vida. Then she cursed under her breath and slammed the door shut.

If it was shaping up to be a standoff between the Gunthers and the Foxworthys, Vida was right. Hand and Vida were the only two people in the room related to both sides. On the one hand the smiling blond Gunthers, Daddy's brothers: easygoing, but loyal. Probably still furious at their dead brother's wife, who had left him and gone back to her maiden name of Foxworthy. On the other hand the Foxxys, as Vida and Hand called them in private: high cheekbones, sinking chins, and "No comment" expressions at any departure from protocol. An example of Upper Crust. Hand had liked visiting his grandparents at their big fancy summer estate in the Hamptons until he had found out how much they hated Daddy.

He knew he should come out. Vida needed him.

But he was still thinking about what had happened when Vida had arrived from Bennington.

His mother parked his father's old bruised Mazda near the drugstore, where the bus dropped off any visitor to Atonquit Falls. There was a teary reunion that Hand, in the backseat, stayed out of. Then his mother dashed into the bank and his sister into the market to shop for groceries, so Hand wandered into the drugstore. He was looking at the greeting-card rack, wondering why they didn't have special cards for "On the Death of Your Husband" or "Now that Papa's Cold and Dead" the way they had "To a Great Nephew on His Tenth Birthday" or "On the Graduation of Your Granddaughter." He was hunched over the rack when the door opened.

It was Mrs. Honeybone, the cafeteria cook at Atherton Academy. She was a well-known gossip, so Hand wasn't surprised to hear her mutter to the clerk, "Well, look-see who's back in town."

"What do you mean by that?" said the clerk. Atonquit Falls was small enough for everyone's comings and goings to be noticed and remarked upon.

"I heard her introduce herself to the bank teller next to me, just a minute ago," said Mrs. Honeybone. "It's Mrs. Gunther. The wife of Rudy Gunther, who died a couple of days ago. You know, Oasis Motel? The sleaziest fleabag in three counties?"

"I know the place, but I never met the guy."

19

"His son Hand found him dead on the floor. Stone cold."

"From what? Did he die, I mean?"

"Well, the official word is heart attack," said Mrs. Honeybone, "but I call it murder."

"What do you mean?"

"I call it a murder by Mrs. Fancypants Gunther. In cold blood. Mr. Gunther was a great friend of Mr. Brown's, and they'd sit and chat in the cafeteria sometimes. You hear a lot if you keep your ears open. When she walked out on her husband and her two kids, it was devastating on all three of them. Now that's more than criminal negligence. In *my* book. She left him to raise those two kids, he who didn't know his ass from his elbow. In *my* book she done it, and she done it in a cold-blooded campaign. I bet she's gloating now."

"Of course you only heard his side of it," said the clerk mildly.

"Kathy," snorted Mrs. Honeybone, "you know this man for five minutes, you know there was no running around, no wife beating, no playing the horses, no drinking yourself blind. He was a quality guy. And look at her out there. Doesn't look like she's mourning to me."

"She doesn't exactly look grief-stricken," agreed the clerk.

"Stand by your man, in the gospel according to Tammy Wynette," said Mrs. Honeybone. "That's my motto. Care to place a bet on how long she'll hang around here for that son of hers? I give it three weeks."

Mrs. Honeybone paid for her purchase, dropped a couple of quarters in the fund-raising jar for war orphans, and marched with self-approval out the door.

How long? Hand wondered, in the dark under the stairs. *How long* would *his mother stay? And what did he want her to do? Stay or go?* He didn't know.

Hand pushed the door open and crabbed his way out of the crawl space. With a feeling of dread he ventured into the main room.

There were sixty or seventy people. On one side stood the Gunther uncles and their wives. Uncle Max and Uncle Emil were laughing, loudly, their big bellies like twenty-pound sacks of flour under their sweat-stained white shirts. The baby of the four brothers, and the only one younger than his father, Uncle Wolfgang had a grim, wiry look. Even though Hand hardly ever saw him, he could tell who Uncle Wolfgang was by the familiar Gunther nylon-string hair and the broad shoulders. Aunt Tess was telling some story and Aunt Barbara was laughing, but they were both dabbing their eyes at the same time. The rest of the room was cowed into silence by the force of their exclusive memories.

Grandma and Grandpa Foxworthy were perched on a loveseat with lips pursed. *What heartache this man brought us*, they seemed to say by their

21

posture and folded hands. *When our daughter married him, we disowned her; we felt we should. Yet how good are we to see our daughter through this final indignity. How charitable.*

Vida was sitting in a chair near them, looking uncomfortable. Hand knew he should go up to the Foxxys and say something, but "Hi Grandma, hi Grandpa," didn't seem very brilliant. He headed that way but his mother's voice hooked him and dragged him off course.

"Hand, darling. Come and say hello—"

His mother was clasping the hands of Mrs. Honeybone, who was squeezed into a black sweater and slacks she'd outgrown by several sizes. She looked like an overweight cat burglar.

"This is someone who works at Atherton," his mother said. Hand nodded as if he'd never seen Mrs. Honeybone before.

The Atherton cook clamped a steel hand on his shoulder. "You be good and strong for your mother," she said in a raspy caw. It was embarrassing— everyone could hear. "You're the man of the family now."

Hand didn't know what to say to this remark. The man of what family?

"You're a good boy, Hand," announced the cook, as if it were classified information and only she had noticed. She turned to his mother. "Now hear me, Mrs. Gunther: you'll find friends in this town." *But not me,* he half expected her to say. *I think you're a real piece of work.* But instead she looked his mother full in the face and said, "It's been a rough road for you and nobody knows it like you do. But you won't go needy in this town. It's that kind of place—we're just like that. We'll miss Rudy more than we can say."

Mrs. Honeybone kept rubbing his mother's hands between her own as if trying to kindle a fire. After a while she wandered off. A minister arrived and began to look official. "Mom," Hand muttered, "Daddy was a Quaker. Did you arrange this?"

"Nobody on the Gunther side takes initiative. It's a family weakness," she answered, "and all I know is how to get a minister. Your father didn't have anything against the Church."

"He wasn't an Episcopal anymore. He never went to services."

"Hand," said his mother, "please."

Just then Ms. Fernald, the chair of the Language Arts Department at Atherton, made her way across the room. Her exuberant hair was knotted severely and bundled in a black net sack on her neck. "Oh boy, now we get Great Quotes of Sorrow," Hand remarked. "Ms. Fernald can't talk without quoting poetry. If Daddy weren't already dead, she'd recite him to death."

His mother said, "Hand, please don't be snide, not today. I can't have it."

What right do you have to say what you can and can't have? he thought. *You made his life miserable by walking out. Everybody is saying it, everyone in town, and they don't even know you. It must show.*

On the day of the funeral, a breathy spring sprinkle blew up into a storm worthy of high summer. It flattened the rich green grass of the cemetery. It tore silk and nylon from umbrellas and cracked their aluminum ribs. It sent ropes of brown water gurgling along the blacktop roadways. The minister cut the prayers short, and the mourners straggled down the slope between the gravestones to their cars. Hand, Vida, and their mother were in a black limo shiny as new shoes. The Gunther brothers and their wives followed in another. Grandma and Grandpa Foxworthy were chauffeured in their Lincoln Continental. Other mourners sprinted for their Toyotas and Hyundais.

Their mother and Vida sat staring out of opposite car windows. Hand had no place to train his eyes except the back of the driver's neck. The strangest feeling of all was the indignity of *leaving* his father at the cemetery. In one part of his mind Hand knew full well that you left the corpse behind, you didn't drag it around with you like luggage, like an old favorite sofa. But Hand felt that if he turned around and looked, he'd see the casket opening. Not like a horror film, not with a ghoulish decomposed demon emerging, but just his father, laughing, saying, "Wait, wait for me, it's just a joke."

He didn't turn around. He did, however, catch

24

the green of the graveyard, in an emerald blur, at an angle in the driver's rearview mirror.

The funeral cortege snaked its way along the river, in the shadow of the shuddering forested Berkshires, then up a small rounded knoll to where the Atherton Academy Trustees' Hall sat aloof.

"What an out-of-the-way place for such a gem of a building," crowed Grandma as she got out of her car and saw the stylish pediment and painted white columns, the high old windows. "Greek Revival, and a fine specimen, too."

"We like it," said Mr. Brown. He took her arm and led her up the granite steps. "It's small, but pretentious."

Uncle Wolfgang laughed at that. Grandma Foxworthy fixed an expression on her face of tolerance wearing through, fast.

The tall window sashes were raised in their frames, and rattled with the green wet wind. The burgundy drapes stirred. Sixth-graders in school uniforms passed trays of sandwiches that looked as if they'd been sat upon. As cars arrived, delivering mourners in droves, the room grew noisier and warmer.

Hand stood, hands jammed in the pockets of his scratchy new black trousers, wishing it were over and everyone gone away. It seemed that everyone here knew what to say, knew what to do, knew how to cry. Hand realized that his ignorance in the situation was normal; he'd never been to a funeral before, much less of anyone related to him. But he had expected somehow that reactions would come naturally: platitudes, sympathy, gratitude, tears. Instead he felt like a foreigner at a party where everyone spoke another language. His instinct for how to *grieve correctly* seemed missing.

When Hand was seven, their cat called Little Accident was run over by a delivery van. He cried for a week. Had he gotten so much less *human* since then? Still, he supposed he could just hang out and eavesdrop on what other people were saying, and hope not to be talked to very much. He had to learn somewhere. And hanging out on the edge of things was his usual way anyhow.

Hand was surprised, a little, at what he heard.

First, there was the gush of praise. Rudy was a saint. Only the good die young. He was a *real* pacifist, not a theorist. He practiced what he preached. He hated injustice. He adored freedom. He adored a double of Johnny Walker Black. (That was Uncle Max, looking sadly at the ladylike helping of white wine in the two-ounce glass.) What I learned from Rudy Gunther! He lives on in his students. He lives on in us all.

It sounded like people remembering a favorite TV show.

"He would sacrifice anything for his ideals," said Ms. Fernald, her eyes bright. "He was an inspiration to have on the faculty." She gripped the strap of her handbag and began to quote. "'The quality of mercy is not strain'd, / It droppeth as the gentle

rain from heaven / Upon the place beneath. . . .'"
This seemed to mean an enormous amount to her,
maybe because it had been raining on the coffin
and was raining still. She had to turn and blow her
nose.

"He would have wanted us to drink his health,"
said Uncle Max. "Emil, go out and find a decent
bottle like a decent brother, will you? This stuff is
piss."

His mother was looking very pale and
composed, linking arms with Vida. Vida was
playing Sisters with her, a thing she used to do
years ago. Tilting her head and leaning on her
mother's shoulder, fiddling with her mother's
scented corn-silk hair. It seemed like a strange
place to take this game up again. Or maybe Vida
was only playing Devoted Daughter, a quick study.

Hand tried to look purposely vague and intent,
as if searching for someone he really wanted to
find, so no one would talk to him. As he circulated
around the room, he realized that he was picking
up as much quiet gossip about his mother as fond
memories of his dad.

She's looking pretty good, isn't she? No flies on
her. Rudy never said a word against her, just his
way, but I bet he was sick about it. She's the type
you don't trust as far as you can throw. And to
think they met on a schoolbus going to a protest in
D.C.? She's money, and you know what *that*
means: once money, always money. Oh sure, her
parents disinherited her for marrying a do-gooder

rabble-rouser, but then she left him. So she's probably rolling in cash.

Then there was Aunt Tess saying stubbornly, "I always liked Clare. You don't judge a book by its cover." Aunt Barbara rolled her eyes and remarked that Aunt Tess was going to turn into the new Rudy Gunther now that the spot was vacant, and be all things to all people.

"*No* one can fill my little brother's shoes," said Uncle Max. "Emil, Wolfgang, let's have a toast." Uncle Max put his drink on the closed lid of the Steinway and struck the glass several times with a pen. "A-hem," said Uncle Max, a real word, not a throat-clearing "a-hem." Grandpa stood up and Grandma looked down. His mother hugged Vida tighter, as if she were afraid she might topple over.

"We all knew Rudolf Gunther in one way or another," said Uncle Max. "He would have wanted us to tell some good stories today, have a laugh or two at his expense. When we were kids in Altoona, he used to sneak into funerals at Saint Casimir's. He used to sit in the back row and pretend to bawl loudly into a handkerchief. He wasn't always Mr. Bleeding Heart—he could enjoy the spectacle people made of themselves. He could laugh at himself, too. There was a lot to laugh at, you got to admit. Come on, you got to admit it."

Uncle Max paused but no one chuckled. It didn't yet seem like a time for laughter.

"When we were in college, he used to drag us off to Appalachia in the summers to build schools for poor mountain kids. He used to say, 'There's only two rules. Number one: Don't sweat the small potatoes. And number two: Everything is small potatoes.'"

"But he lived as if everything were urgent," said Uncle Wolfgang, not arguing but not agreeing either. "Peace Corps even when it was no longer fashionable. Amnesty International. Helping to raise money for refugee resettlement from Southeast Asia. The works."

"He got through his trials," said Uncle Max broadly. "And in the end death was good to him. It came swift and sure, no pussyfooting around. Let's drink to the man who never let himself get mown down, not by anything. Not by any of the troubles, and he had many, believe me—"

"Hear, hear," intoned Grandpa Foxworthy. "Cheers." He made a show of sipping his wine. Grandma followed suit, and so did everyone else, and then Uncle Max couldn't revive his train of thought. The social buzz swarmed in again and the public moment was over.

Hand leaned against a pillar and listened to the eulogies. It sounded as if people were nominating Rudy Gunther for sainthood. He knew why. *Peace* had been his father's big obsession. Not for nothing had he named his daughter Davida—after Henry David Thoreau. And *Hand* was for Mohandas Gandhi Gunther.

And if *Hand* had been an offbeat nickname in New Haven, Connecticut, and Radley, Massachusetts, it was even more so in Atonquit Falls. The run-down Oasis Motel excepted, Atonquit Falls was everybody's choice for Main Street, U.S.A. With the pretty-as-a-picture rocking chairs on spruced-up porches. Houses painted a glaring, granulated-sugar white, and hedges only as high as the Village Historical Association would allow. (Hand's dad, who didn't mind much about overgrown hedges, had called them the Village Hysterical Association.) Even the color of shutters and front doors was a matter of public debate.

Hand saw Letitia Brown coming toward him with two cups of punch. He was glad for her concern, but he didn't want to let her down by having nothing to say. Trying to seem casual, he looked around and saw his Uncle Wolfgang, who sat straddling a folding chair backward as if at a card game. Hand sidled up and said, "Mind if I sit down?"

"Be my guest," said Uncle Wolfgang.

Hand didn't know Uncle Wolfgang well. He lived in Atlanta and did something in stage design. Hand usually saw Aunt Tess, Uncle Max, Aunt Barbara, and Uncle Emil on Cape Cod for a week every summer, but Uncle Wolfgang never came to that.

"We don't see you very often," said Hand, thinking if he got the conversation going on Uncle Wolfgang, he'd be safe from prying questions.

"If not for times like this, it would be never," said Uncle Wolfgang.

"Hmmm," he said, as if there were a lot of unspoken opinion behind the syllable.

The noise in the room increased. Wine was still flowing liberally. Collars were being loosened and tie knots being inched lower. Handbags were deposited on windowsills. Ms. Fernald had stepped out of her high heels and was rubbing her arches on the rung of a metal chair.

"Will you miss your brother?" asked Hand, trying out how everyone else talked to *him*.

"Will you miss your father?" Uncle Wolfgang shot back. For a person in a relaxed position, his retort came like a volley from an Uzi.

Hand flinched.

"Sorry," said Uncle Wolfgang. "Of course I'll miss him. The good brother. The good soul." He sighed.

"I'm not prying," said Hand.

"Sure you are. I would too if I weren't so tired."

"Tired?"

"Exhausted." He blinked. His eyes were rheumy and red. "So are you. You just don't notice it yet."

"Tired of what?"

"Tired of polite conversation. Tired of the strain of keeping correct. I don't want to offend Clare or her parents. I do upset them—we all do—merely by looking like Rudy. That kind of tension takes its toll, you know."

Hand knew about that. He nodded.

"Did you come straight from Atlanta?" Hand asked.

"Oh, I was already in Massachusetts," said Uncle Wolfgang. "I had flown up here to go to Amherst and look over Emily Dickinson's house. The

31

company I freelance for is putting on *The Belle of Amherst*, and I'm doing prelims for the set. Thank God I called and got my messages, or I might've gone back home before finding out about Rudy."

"You were in Massachusetts already?"

"Flew into Bradley, rented a car. Listened to my tape of the Aaron Copland/Emily Dickinson song cycle. The irony, Hand! 'I felt a Funeral, in my Brain, / And Mourners to and fro / Kept treading—treading—till it seemed / That sense was breaking through—' I can't hum the Copland for you, it's impossible. But death was on my mind all week. So much of Dickinson is about dying."

"Yeah," said Hand, but he didn't want to talk about dying, or about poetry.

"Ah, the irony," said Wolfgang again. He brushed a fly away. He was a handsome man. With his super-stylish haircut he looked like a model in a cologne ad. His green eyes glinted gold; his gaze was inward. The fly circled his blond head. "'I heard a Fly buzz—when I died—'" he said. "Sheez, I've had too much wine. I shouldn't be quoting Dickinson at you."

"Why haven't we seen more of you?" Hand was trying out phrases he'd been hearing the grown-ups use. "You shouldn't be such a stranger."

"Ah, stranger than most," said Uncle Wolfgang.

"Didn't you and Daddy get along?"

"He got along with everybody, Hand."

"Do you?"

Uncle Wolfgang laughed. "Oh, I'm a much

32

crankier guy. I'm easily disappointed in people."
He shrugged, held his shoulders up a moment
before dropping them. "I did admire Rudy. All that
high energy directed at perfecting a lousy world.
But he was a hard act to follow, growing up. I got
all the temper that he never developed. His
winning ways, they used to irk me. But enough
about me; how do *you* feel?"

The question of the hour. Hand pretended he
hadn't heard it, because he didn't know the
answer. Instead he blathered, "I'm sure Daddy
loved you."

"He did," said Uncle Wolfgang blandly. "If I'd
been a stranger getting in his way in the parking
lot he'd've loved me. I could hardly feel very
special, could I, since his love was so blanket and
universal? He wasn't even that smart, you know.
He was just constant."

Hand was beginning to feel uncomfortable. But
before he could escape, Uncle Wolfgang had
grabbed him by the wrist.

"It'll hit you later, Hand," he said. "'The bustle in
the house the morning after death. . . .' You'll feel
it later, you should know that, if you don't feel it
now. I know you don't know what to say, you
don't know what to feel. That's normal. But you'll
need someone to talk things over with. Take my
card. Go on, take it—I am your uncle, after all.
Give me a call if you need to chat."

"Okay," said Hand.

He barreled out of the parlor looking for a place

to be alone. He ran halfway up the marble steps to the landing and flung himself down on the cushioned windowseat.

He felt he could hear his father's voice. What his father would have to say about all this! *I hate all this blarney; people who spend time praising other people who don't need it are taking time away from real jobs that need to be done.* He would be grinning, tousling Hand's hair, or slapping him on the arm lightly, affectionately. Hand would be grinning back, even if he didn't agree. *Sometimes you need to hear it, even if it's blarney,* he would've liked to say back to his father. *Sometimes praising other people is a real job that needs to be done. People aren't all as sure of themselves as you are, Daddy.*

Were.

The image of the grinning man, scorning compliments, faded from Hand's mind like the Cheshire Cat: body first, then face, then smile, and last the light in his eyes. In its place the rain drove ripples of distorting water down the window glass. It rained over the playing fields, it gurgled in the gutters and spouts, no doubt it splashed on the mahogany coffin out there in the green burial meadow, where nobody waited to keep watch.

⟶ three ⟵

The day after the funeral was weird. Hand wandered from one room to the next looking for something to do. His mother seemed to be chained to the telephone, or forever brewing tea for some visitor or other. The uncles and aunts hung around, getting in the way, trying to help. It was a relief when they finally left—as if things could get back to normal. But what was normal?

Uncle Wolfgang was the last to go. He threw his bag into the back of the rented car and turned to say good-bye. "You know it'll get worse before it gets better," he said to Hand. "It takes a long time to understand something like this."

How the hell do you know? Hand wanted to say. And maybe he was sulking pretty obviously, because it was as if Uncle Wolfgang had heard him. His uncle said, "Don't forget your Grandpa Gunther died—and he was *my* dad."

So what? thought Hand.

"I've had other loved ones die, too," said Uncle Wolfgang.

Hand didn't know why he was being so sulky. He noticed, however, that Vida gave Uncle Wolfgang a huge hug. Vida had been hobnobbing with Uncle Wolfgang. Maybe that was it. Maybe he felt left out. "Take care of yourself," said Vida breathily to their uncle. "There's never enough family at a time like this!"

As if I'm not enough? thought Hand. *Sheez, give me a break from your Hollywood-style heartache.*

Their mother shook hands coolly, deliberately. "Good-bye, Wolfgang. Drive carefully."

Uncle Wolfgang flung himself into the car. "When you can manage it, go away for a day or two," he said. "It's good to get away. And you'll find that coming home is not easy. It makes you realize more than ever that he's not here. But it helps you to feel that, too; you have to get used to it."

"We'll do what we think best," said their mother in an even voice. They watched the car leave. "As if nobody's ever lost a loved one before," she said, almost under her breath.

"Oh well," said Vida hotly, "you can't deny it: He knows death by heart, just about—"

"Enough," said their mother. *She shouldn't have the authority to quiet us down—not when she'd walked out three years ago!* thought Hand.

The three of them stood in the parking lot, waiting for life to begin again.

"Come on, you two," said their mother suddenly, a forced cheeriness. "Buck up. Maybe your uncle is right. Let's throw a suitcase together and go off for a day. There'll be plenty of time ahead to grieve—"

"Right *now*? You're not serious!" Vida was shocked. She pulled down the fake granny glasses she wore and peered over the tops like an old prude. "And Daddy not a week dead yet? I'm not going anywhere! It isn't—it isn't *right*!"

"There's no right and wrong in grieving," said their mother calmly. "Let's get back on the right footing. We need a day together—the three of us. Tragedy or not."

"You can't make me!" said Vida.

"I need a little more readjustment time than I've had," said their mother as she headed for the screen door. "I'm asking you to humor me. In this instance, what would your father have wanted you to do?"

Bested, Vida whistled and looked at Hand. "Well, come on, little kiddo, we're stuck with Mrs. Family Togetherness. Might as well grin and bear it."

Hand said, "I might have a track meet tomorrow. I'll tell her I can't go."

"Good luck," said Vida. "Bet you a buck it doesn't work."

◄◄◄▶►►

An hour later the three of them were in their father's old car. Vida had spread herself all over the backseat, so Hand was stuck in the front with their mother. She seemed determined to be upbeat, as if three years ago she hadn't walked out on them. *How can she pretend she never left?* thought Hand. Even though she had wanted to take them with her, they hadn't wanted to go. And she hadn't fought to keep them with her, either. She'd accepted their scared, wobbly-voiced decision. She'd told them that they were always welcome to visit, and had even offered to send them money. Vida *had* visited once, but she'd said precious little about it when she came back. And Hand hadn't asked much, either.

"Burger King or Kentucky Fried for lunch?" asked their mother.

"I'm not hungry," said Vida.

"Pizza," said Hand.

"Are you okay for pizza, Vida?"

"I'll eat it but I won't enjoy it." But Hand could tell Vida was lightening up. She was going to make a game out of being sulky, just as she had made a game out of being a college girl. She didn't have any real responses—they were all poses. She was always auditioning for something in her head.

Over a large pepperoni and mushrooms, their mother finally got around to asking them questions about their lives. It was like an interrogation by the Gestapo. School. Friends. This. That. Hand answered in the shortest phrases he could. Vida lied extravagantly. "I know you missed me," said their mother at one point, working the conversation around to the three of them.

38

"Missed you?" said Vida. "We hated you. We loved you. We still do."

"I'm going to the bathroom; too much root beer," said Hand.

By the time he got back, Vida had dropped the last of her ditzy changeable personalities. She and their mother were talking quietly, glancing at each other warmly and looking quickly away. Their voices faded when he got to the table. "So Hand," said Vida, "we were trying to figure out where to go."

"Vermont?" said their mother. "Or maybe we could go to Connecticut? It's up to you."

"Or Cape Cod," said Vida.

"I thought you didn't want to come, Vida," said Hand, slumping into his seat.

"You don't sound very excited," said Vida disapprovingly. "How about the Baseball Hall of Fame? You always wanted to go there."

"I wanted to go there with *Daddy*," said Hand.

"Cooperstown it is—why not?" said their mother, getting up to pay.

"Vida," he spat, "you're a real traitor."

"What," she said, "I can't talk to my own mother because my father died?"

"It's not Daddy you're betraying, it's me."

"Oh yeah, how?"

But he couldn't say how; it wasn't exactly clear. It was just that by the time they got back in the car, the balance had changed. It was now a car full of female thought and feelings and there wasn't any room for him. He closed his eyes and pretended to be asleep.

By the time they arrived in Cooperstown, New York, Vida and their mother had bonded like Super Glue. He purposely straggled behind them as they went parading down the sidewalk. He felt less like a boy and more like a dog every minute.

His mother stayed resolutely bright spirited. "Come on, Champ, lose the glum face. We're doing this for you." They had foot-long hot dogs for dinner at a sidewalk vendor's cart, and when Vida took a bite of hers and a squirt of watery mustard jetted onto their mother's jacket, they all laughed. But Hand could tell he was laughing for the wrong reasons.

⋘⋙

The next morning Vida wanted to wash her hair and lounge around the motel room, which was so much fancier than the Oasis rooms that it made Hand feel ashamed. So he and his mother went off to the Hall of Fame by themselves.

He tried to tell himself that she was being nice, real nice. She even left him alone, so he could look at the exhibits in peace. But in reality he could hardly read the words. Daddy had meant to take him here. He'd said any number of times that he would. What was his mother doing here instead? It was so unfair. Life was unfair. Life was unfair and his mother was an intruder and Vida was a traitor.

"Hey, let's check the gift shop—I bet there's something you'd like there," said his mother. "You can spend up to ten dollars if you find something cool."

Hearing her say *something cool,* as if she thought she and he were the same age! Well, maybe it was meant to make him feel close to her, but it had the opposite effect. A *million* miles away by now, and racing farther and farther away every second.

"You don't want anything?" she said after he'd glanced over the displays and walked on.

"It's all junk," he said.

They headed in silence toward the motel. He didn't mind not talking, but he guessed it bugged his mother, because after a while she said softly, "You're not trying, Hand. You're really not trying to enjoy this."

"I'm enjoying it just fine."

"Maybe this was a stupid idea. But I'm glad we have a chance to be together. I've missed you, you know. I realize how I've been blocking it—how much I missed you all along."

Yeah, right, he thought. *Thanks for telling me.*

"Even if you don't want to talk about it, I'm sure you missed me," she said. "I don't blame you for being confused. It must have been hard for you."

"I'm not confused, I'm tired," he said. "My feet always hurt in museums."

"I know, mine too," she said. "Isn't it strange? I

can walk for three hours without stopping, but half an hour in a museum and I feel twenty years older. I wonder why that is."

He didn't know and didn't care and didn't answer.

"Twenty years older than I should feel," she murmured, but by now she didn't seem to expect an answer.

◄◄--►►

The drive home was even worse. Vida and his mother began to sing. Vida could carry a tune all right, but his mother had a singing voice that only a child young enough for lullabies could bear.

"Come on, Hand, you like to sing," said Vida more than once. "What about the theme song for the Addams Family? Dunh duh duh duh, click click . . ."

"Stop it, Vida. You're making me carsick," he said. He had commandeered the backseat this time, and lay down so his head wasn't even in the rearview mirror.

"Are you really feeling sick, Hand?" asked his mother. "Shall I pull over?"

"Oh, please, don't pay any attention," said Vida. "You know, Hand, this stupid sulking is really annoying. You're not sick."

Hand threw up all over the backseat. It was disgusting, of course, but he was sort of pleased with the timing.

42

◄◄┄►►

When they got back to the Oasis, it was almost dark. And Uncle Wolfgang had been right. Hand felt the absence of his father more than ever. It was almost like a horror film where someone gets sucked out of life, right through the walls, out into nowhere and nothingness. His father was missing in the most present, palpable, bothering kind of way.

Hand heard his mother and his sister saying good night to each other, heard the smack of their kisses on each other's cheeks. He wasn't sure how much he trusted Vida, she of the drama class and comedy improv clubs. Yet the welcome she was giving their mother seemed generous enough. And in return she was getting more back from their mother than he was.

Of course, he thought, rolling over, punching his pillow harder than he needed to, Vida had never lived here with their father the way he had. She'd gone off to college last September, and he and his dad hadn't moved into the Oasis until December. So she wouldn't feel the loss in the same way. For her the reunion with their mother was poignant and timely. Vida didn't feel their father in every nook and cubbyhole of this old motor court. What did she know of the shape of their father's absence in these mildewy rooms, under these decaying eaves?

⊷ four ↠

A week after the funeral Hand got a postcard from Uncle Wolfgang. The picture was an old-fashioned photo portrait, in sepias, a stern woman's face, fundamental as oak and yet fiery even after all this time.

Dear Hand,

I was quoting some Dickinson, probably getting it wrong. Was it this one?

The Bustle in a House
The Morning after Death
Is solemnest of industries
Enacted upon Earth—

The Sweeping up the Heart
And putting Love away
We shall not want to use again
Until Eternity.

Grim. Honest. Keep in touch if you like. These are hard times for you, Hand. I've been through them before. I know.

As ever, Wolfgang.

As ever? Hand wondered. *As ever* what?

He pinned the card on the office bulletin board. Maybe the poem was right about the days following a death. The small house tacked onto the back of the motel office and reception room was in a state of bustle it had never seen under Rudy Gunther's management. Every morning his mother got herself into jeans, a black-and-gold scarf wrapping her hair, and began to fire off assignments. "Years of grime in this dump," she kept muttering. "Whether we stay or go, it's got to be clean."

The regular tenants were two old sisters, the Misses Formsby; a taciturn security guard named Marvin Small; and a county health aide, Polly Chaucer. Safety in numbers, they trooped into the office Saturday at noontime to talk with their new landlady about the motel. They wanted to ask her some questions. Was she going to sell it? Remodel it? Develop it and kick them out? (At this possibility the Misses Formsby blinked rapidly, in unison.) In fact, said Polly Chaucer bravely, did Clare Foxworthy actually *have* any legal claim to the Oasis? Not to overstep the bounds of taste and upset her in her period of mourning, but *was* Clare in fact Rudy's legal heir or merely his ex-wife?

45

Vida and Hand made to step out, but their mother, with the motion of a finger, halted them in their tracks.

"If our lodgers are curious about this, you must be, too," she said. "Rudy Gunther and I were never divorced—nor even legally separated. This doesn't mean he mightn't have made a new will." She pointed to a mound of newspapers, manila folders, papers, catalogues, Styrofoam plates with dried pizza and little red ants crawling on the crusts, phone books. "His filing system is capricious."

"Oh," said Polly Chaucer. Marvin Small bit his lip and waited. The ancient Misses Formsby tried to defend their former landlord. "He was such a good—" "Such a good man, Edith means—" "—A good *motel* administrator, Frances—" "Of course. A fine—" "—And we'd never—" "Of course we always—" "—But sooner or later—"

"He was a *slob*," said Hand's mother.

"Cleanliness is next to godliness but on the downward slope," sniffed Miss Edith Formsby. Her sister glared in surprise at a full sentence.

"We'll keep you posted," said their mother. "The minute we've determined the status of this place, you'll know. We're very grateful for your concern."

"We like it here," said Marvin Small suddenly. His gray hair fell in a single thin lock like an old-fashioned typewriter key across his forehead. "We want to stay."

"I understand. Now if you'll excuse us? Hand, bring the stepladder, and Vida, we'll need some more garbage bags, also more detergent." The delegation single-filed itself away.

Hand didn't know how Vida felt about it, but he was grateful to go to the store, freed for a while from relentless change.

Vida found a parking space on Greylock Street but had to do a lot of wheel twisting and neck craning to get into it. Hand thought she was concentrating single-mindedly on her driving, and when she said, "Well, Hand, what did you make of Mom's bombshell today?" he was taken aback, and simply said, "Don't know. What do you think?"

"Do you think it's true? That they never got a divorce?"

Sitting in a small enclosed space with a person of Vida's cayenne opinions made him itch to get out. "Let's go get the groceries," he said.

"I asked you a question. Aren't you listening?"

"How should I know?" said Hand. "I didn't like to talk to Daddy about it because I didn't want to get him upset."

Vida said, "I suppose I should have found out myself. But Mom didn't want to talk about it to me, and I always thought that Daddy was confiding in *you*. I didn't want to butt in. You should have *asked* him, Hand. Now it's too late to know how he felt. If you don't ask any questions you'll never get any answers."

"You're pals with Mom—why don't *you* ask her now? You yak all night long and I can't get to sleep. Besides," said Hand, "you've got someplace to go back to when this is all over. What about me?"

"Well, follow your current campaign of silence and *don't ask any questions*; then it'll all come as a nice big surprise." Vida hurled herself through the supermarket door, snatched up a cart, and barreled down the produce aisle in a royal snit. There wasn't any point trying to catch up, not when she was in one of her moods. So Hand hung out near the community bulletin board and did a series of hamstring stretches.

Eventually Vida came through the line. Hand reached out to take one of the bags of groceries, but she hugged both to her chest.

On the way back, Hand said, "Vida, I can't figure out whether they could have gotten divorced or not. I thought about it but I just don't know."

Vida relented but said righteously, "It's our business to know these things now, Hand. I certainly have mixed feelings about Mom, just like you have. Some of it is resentment. She *did* leave us, Hand. But we're stuck with her as a mother, so we might as well accept her and get on with it."

Are we stuck with her, or is she stuck with us? Hand wondered, but he only said, "We could have gone with her."

"Right-o," she said, by which he figured she meant it was nobody's fault, so hugs and kisses all around, and forget three years of pain his mother had caused—for their father, for Vida, and for him, too.

Vida switched on the radio, maybe so they wouldn't have to talk about it any more. He was glad she did, though he changed the station to something less middle-aged and mellow.

When they pulled into the unpaved yard that served as the parking lot, they saw barrels and boxes and plastic garbage bags set out under the motel's tired neon sign. Their mom had gone into warp drive while they were shopping. Hand suddenly thought: What of Daddy's is she throwing out?

She paused in her work when Hand appeared in the doorway of his father's room. His dad's clothes were piled up on the bed. His dresser drawers hung open. The closet was empty but for some wire hangers. "You're back," said his mother, "just in time."

"You can't do this, Mom!" Hand hardly knew what he was saying. "You don't have any right. You left him, and this is his stuff, not yours."

"I'm just doing my job," she said roughly. She pulled open another drawer and reached in with determined hands. It was a pile of handwritten pages torn out of a notebook, and a handful of old photographs, and underneath that a dirty magazine. She made a choking sound and threw the magazine into the trash as if it were crawling with bugs.

"Don't you go lecturing me, Mohandas! I had enough patronizing from your father. I don't like this any more than you do, but I'll do what needs to be done!" With the photos and notebook pages in her hands, she pushed past him down the hall to the mildewy bathroom. He heard the faucet run, hard.

Hand worked fast. He stuffed his pockets with anything and everything—cufflinks, gum, foreign coins, a money clip. He thought about salvaging the magazine, too, but he resisted. By the time his mother came out, he was through and had gone into the office.

"I'll tell you one thing, Hand Gunther," she said in a voice that sounded as if she'd been telling him for fifteen minutes of practice in the bathroom. "You are entitled to your opinion of me. I'm your mother and I faced a hard choice and I made it. I lived with it and I'll live with your disapproval if I have to. I don't like this any more than you do. But do you see his brothers here helping me? No you don't. The only decent part of all this is that it brought me back to you and Vida." Her voice got steely. "Letting you two stay behind was the hardest thing I ever did."

Hand didn't look at her. She waited, then said, "I'm going to go start supper. Did you get the vegetables?"

"Vida put them in the fridge."

"All right." She was so quiet that Hand thought she'd left and he made the mistake of looking up. "All right?" she said again, softly.

"All right, Mom," he answered in a monotone, rolling his eyes at the opposite wall. The postcard

Hand had gotten from Uncle Wolfgang stared at him from the bulletin board. He read it over. "These are hard times for you, Hand. Don't forget I've been through them before. I know." He began to think about how odd it was that Uncle Wolfgang had been in Amherst, Massachusetts, the week his father died. Amherst wasn't very far from Atonquit Falls; why then had he not come by for a visit? Or had he?

"Dinner," called his mother, in peace-making tones, but Hand's stomach had given up for the time being. He fiddled with his food, and then he excused himself saying he had to train. He laced up his Reeboks and shook out his kinks, warmed up, and then headed out for a five-mile run.

The blue jays screamed their news bulletins. A car passed him. Hand was running through swarms of evening midges. Running along the Buxton road to where Stone Farm Road branched off. Swinging his arms and tasting the willpower in his saliva.

He ran to escape the thoughts of Mom trashing Daddy's room.

He made the gradual slope near Smith's roadside stand, where the road leveled off between low, tumbling fieldstone walls. A black shape suddenly tore itself out of a tree and fell purposefully toward him, screeching. Then another, and two, three more. In the honeyed air five huge crows came whirring on him, beating their big wings and cawing at him. One pecked his ear. Hand cried out and scissored his arms about.

But the crows kept diving at him, croaking and crying. By the time they left, Hand was nearly weeping with fright. He knew no one would believe him. He hardly believed it himself. *It really happened,* he found himself thinking, on every panting breath, over and over, *it really did happen.*

The sun poured amber through the black pines. Hand was more alone than ever before in his life.

Part Two

To break so vast a Heart
Required a Blow as vast—
No Zephyr felled this Cedar straight—
'Twas undeserved Blast—

five

Things were settling down some. Time carried on no matter how anyone felt. Vida went back to Bennington. The lilacs by the Dumpster came out. The Atherton track team won several events at the last two invitationals of the year. The coroner's report finally arrived in a manila envelope. Acute cardiac failure. The exact time of death wasn't reported, just "afternoon." Hand watched his mother look at it, then put it aside. "How accurate do you think this is?" he asked.

"Hand, it's a formality," she said, and went to get a Tylenol.

The tulips went by. The roses came out. Weeks creaked past.

Mom talked to Mr. Brown and arranged that Hand could continue at Atherton, tuition-free, at least until he graduated from middle school—two more years. This was done without her asking Hand whether he wanted to.

Now that his father was dead, she was making a choice to waltz back in and play parent at the crunch. Over breakfast one day she said, slapping the newspaper with the back of her hand, "I don't really know what a person's supposed to live on out here in bucolia. This motel doesn't break even, and there's hardly a single job on offer paying more than minimum wage." Hand shrugged. He didn't know either. He remembered that his wealthy grandparents had more or less disinherited his mother, but now that Rudy Gunther was dead, why didn't they loosen up their wallets a little in their daughter's direction? His mother went on, "I'll be behind the counter at McDonald's in Buxton before the year's out, you can put money on it. Me with my education and resumé." She tossed the newspaper into the trash.

Hand left for school, giving up on looking at the sports page. What was he supposed to say? *Sorry, Mom, sorry I live in this small town with few jobs for professionals, sorry that you inherited Daddy's motel.* He had no clue. He said nothing.

Meanwhile, the Great Casserole Flood showed no sign of abating. Casseroles are a phase in the grieving process, Hand wanted to say to Ms. Fernald when she began to lecture him on the Stages of Grief. Denial, Anger, Bargaining, Depression, Acceptance, and, somewhere in there, Casseroles.

Ms. Fernald made him come into her cramped office, and shut the door behind him. Books stacked on books fallen over books heaped on books. A poster of a bust of Shakespeare, and a black-and-white photo of Virginia Woolf. A line drawing of Emily Dickinson. A color snapshot of Ms. Fernald in Stratford-upon-Avon, standing next to someone dressed up in Elizabethan costume. Hand felt crowded by literature.

"You're in denial," Ms. Fernald clucked at him. "Don't get stuck in denial, Hand. Let yourself go."

"I'm not in anything," Hand said, trying to explain, but it came out sounding like ordinary rudeness.

"I have your best interests at heart," she said, fussing with a big pad of Post-it notes, sticking and unsticking the top one compulsively. "Your dad would have wanted me to see that you got through this okay. And Hand, the faculty is worried about your sleepwalking through this hard time of transition. You have to face up to what has happened. You have to feel it."

He didn't like the idea of the faculty discussing him. "I don't think about it a lot," he said. "I don't see why anyone else should. I mean he was *my* father."

"*Exactly*," she said, making a point, but it escaped him. And then he gave an excuse and escaped her smothering concern.

Was he in denial? Hand tried to envision denial noodle casserole on his way to his next class.

Settling in his seat over a biology quiz, he tried to focus on multiple choice questions about cells. The diagrams were like paisleys. He dawdled over them with a pencil, trying to concentrate, but he couldn't focus very well. Was there anything in what Ms. Fernald had said? Denial? What was he denying? That his father had died? He didn't deny that. Hadn't life changed more than he'd ever have guessed possible? What he was denying, maybe, was how lonely it made him. How distant he was from his mother, how suspicious of her he was. With Vida away at Bennington. And his mother driving Number 2 pencils across acres of yellow lined paper, preparing questions for the endless meetings with lawyers, bankers, county clerks, and the like.

What he needed was a friend. But the boys of Atherton were a hard crowd to crack, even after half a year with them. And the death of his father had made them even more reserved than before. Hand felt he was slipping into the category of Rogue Nerd without any real qualifications for it.

Ms. Fernald called him to her office again, a couple of days later. She seemed nothing if not determined. "We're aware that this is a colossal crisis for you, Hand," she breathed. "One parent dying, and the other returning from oblivion— either half of that would be traumatic to the most stable soul." In the poster behind her, William Shakespeare with his domed head looked wry and exhausted at her efforts. Ms. Fernald perched herself on her desk and hummed something about a support group.

"I don't want to join a bunch of losers," said Hand. "I don't need to discuss anything. With anybody."

"I disagree, but I won't arrange it until you ask me to."

"It's just life," he said. "So my father died. So what? Everybody dies. And I'm getting used to Mom again. What choice do I have anyway?"

"You need a peer group. I've watched you withdraw. It's perfectly normal," she hurried on, "and there's no need to be sensitive about it. You're not *alone*, Hand. I'm here for you. I'll be around all summer doing curriculum development, except for some time in early July. Call on me. Call me."

"All right, Ms. Fernald," he said, but he knew he wouldn't.

So he just waited, and the school year came to an end.

One afternoon at the beginning of July, his mom told Hand that over the long Fourth of July holiday weekend she was leaving. For a few seconds his lungs felt tight in his chest, though whether this was relief or panic he couldn't tell. She elaborated, saying she was flying to Seattle to pack up her life and ship it back east. She might be gone a week, maybe more; it was hard to tell how long it would take.

"I'll call from time to time," she said. "But you'll be okay alone?"

"I won't be alone. I've got the old Misses Formsby. They're a laugh and a half."

"I'm asking you a question," she said. "Will you be okay? Do you want to stay at Atherton till I get back? There must be a summer program there. You wouldn't be alone."

"Summer program hasn't started yet. I'll be fine."

She fixed herself a cup of tea. "I don't want you stewing. You seem to have a tendency to moon about," she said. "I wish you weren't so private. I suppose it's a stage you're going through."

Life is a stage I'm going through, he thought, but said nothing.

"You're not listening," said Clare. "I'm telling you: Call this number if there's an emergency." She pushed a business card across the table at him. It read *David Jenkins, Esquire.* "He's my legal counsel."

"David Jenkins," he said. Odd how people kept thrusting cards at him. "Okay."

For several days Hand kept assuring her that everything would be okay. He would be able to handle a holiday crowd if they were lucky enough to get one. He could call David Jenkins, Esquire, if there was trouble. He didn't mind being alone.

"I could just pack you up and take you out west, you know," said Clare distractedly, putting a bag in the trunk of the car. "If things don't work out here, maybe we'll have to do that."

Hand didn't know why she was rooting up her life for him now. He didn't really want to know. He just wanted her to leave, and finally, she did.

Once her perfume had faded from the sunny kitchen, and the earthy spice of geraniums reemerged, Hand got up and took off his Reeboks and padded, barefoot and resolute, to the narrow room she'd taken as her own.

Just as he had guessed, he found the pages of Rudy's handwriting in a drawer.

He spread them out and began to read.

> "A diary is an assassin's cloak which we wear when we stab a comrade in the back with a pen."
>
> —Wm. Soutar, 1898–1943

To refrain from stabbing. To keep from stabbing her. Verbally. To keep clear of projecting blame. Shall you become an assassin now, at this late hour. When you've stood by her as date, mate, lover, touchstone.

To hold her image in focus even though she's gone 5 wks. now.

Will you rewrite the whole story of your marriage to predict this catastrophe.

To hold her face clear in your mind. Clare—

She is absent from the neck up, an expressionless smudge. Trim, angry, shackled with self-control from the neck down.

Vida. How'll she manage. And Hand. How could she leave. He's at that dim sensitive age, untrained in subtlety. He—

It wasn't the "untrained in subtlety" part that stopped Hand. It was just reading about himself in

Daddy's handwriting. Like getting a letter from a dead person, only the Hand that his father was writing about was dead, too. Or at least gone, gone three years now.

> . . . untrained in subtlety. He thinks she's on vacation.
> It's a shutdown, meltdown, foldup thing. Whereas Vida is all spunk and spit. She knows enough to be angry, which is good and healthy for her even if misguided. She'll come out okay. But Hand? And yourself?
> Who's to blame. Is it you. Can you accept it if it is. Can you live with it. (Do you have a choice.) Are you: blind. stubborn. theoretical. cold.
> Can you keep Clare clear as she is, whole and human, intact and in view. Not to diminish her with a latter-day diagnosis of paranoia and selfishness. . . .
> To remember her, say, at Christmas, in New Haven. When the F's came. All exuberant, the baby at her breast, a skillet in one hand with corn bread sizzling and her briefcase propping the French doors open, and the lit tree beyond it in the sunroom. Vida in her cowgirl outfit. Not a still life. Not a still life.

At this point the color of ink changed and Hand

put the paper down. It was maybe one page out of twelve, and he was exhausted by it. He remembered Daddy telling him about the Christmas the F's came—the Foxxys—and how Vida had insisted that the crèche consisted of Joseph, Mary, and the Holy Baby Vida. Baby Hand, she told everyone decisively, had ridden away on the back of a camel. Which showed how she was about having a new member in the family.

> On top of it all—this profound sense of failure. Max and Tess, and Emil and Barbara, not understanding. It's your fault—what did you do wrong, they say. Even Wolfgang, critical as a cop. Where does he get off having an opinion on *marriage*? You say things you don't mean, slam the phone on him. The damage is done. It compounds, it rolls out from you like waves. How will it affect Hand and Vida?

There was Uncle Wolfgang! Critical as a cop! His father slamming the phone on him? Being *angry*? It was hard to imagine.

When the phone rang, shrill as glass shattering, Hand bolted across the room, knocking over a chair. He was sure it was his mother calling from the road somewhere, to give him a last-minute order: "NO PRYING IN MY THINGS."

But it was Ms. Fernald, asking to speak with his

mom. Hand was afraid she was going to bring her campaign to get him therapy right into his own home, and he was glad he could say honestly that his mother wasn't there. He didn't mention she'd gone out of state for an indefinite period.

Ms. Fernald was flummoxed. She was about to leave on a two-week vacation. A couple of refugees from Iran had showed up at the school looking for Hand's father. They had a letter of invitation from him.

"What are they called?" said Hand.

"It's a Mr. Nur Ziba and his little boy, Vuffy."

Hand remembered about this. His dad had mentioned them, what, six weeks ago? Two Iranian immigrants passing through western Massachusetts. "Yes, Dad had intended them to stay here," said Hand. "He was involved with Amnesty International and refugee resettlement leagues. In Radley we had people in sleeping bags on the floor of the living room all the time."

"Well, they seem like nice people, but I don't think I should bring them over without your mother's say-so. Would you look in your father's files and find somebody else on the refugee resettlement committee who could vouch for them?"

"I wouldn't know where to look," said Hand. He was annoyed at the idea that something his father had planned was now subject to approval by his mother, who wasn't even around to veto it. "You know, Ms. Fernald, my father meant for them to stay here. It'll be all right. Really."

"They don't have much money." Ms. Fernald sounded worried. "You say you know them?"

"I know about them."

"I hope your mom is all right with this. She'll be back shortly, you say? I have to come out there within a half hour or I'll miss my plane."

"She won't be home soon. But come right over. No sweat. It'll be okay."

He thought of the grave on the hill, the sunlight on the grass. He could hear his dad's advice: *Action, Hand: It's action that counts.* Well, Daddy, this is action. I'm only carrying it out in your name.

⊷ six ⊷

Ms. Fernald got out of her car. She was wearing a sweatshirt that had on its front the words *Women's Literary Forum and Terrorist League.* Her hair looked as if it were on steroids, fluffed up around her head in airy cumulus masses.

"Here's the letter of introduction," she said, "and this certainly sounds like Rudy, I'll tell you. You're sure your mother is going to be okay about this?"

"Sure I'm sure."

She handed over a piece of paper, folded so many times that the creases were worn thin. It was Atherton Academy stationery, fancy cream-colored stock with curlicued typeface announcing the address. The date was obliterated by a fold.

Dear Mr. Ziba:

The Western Massachusetts Chapter of the Council of Churches, of which I'm the local contact for refugee affairs, has forwarded to me your open letter asking for hospitality on your trip through the eastern U.S. While to date our work in refugee matters has been confined to immigrants from Nicaragua and El Salvador, with an occasional influx of Cambodians, I'll be more than happy to do my part to help you effect your family reunion. When you're in the final leg of your trip to Boston, you must feel free to come by the Oasis Motel in Atonquit Falls. I'll find you a room and make further arrangements for your trip to Boston. I understand there's a Muslim community there with whom you'll be welcome. My regards to the Ismaili jamat of Cleveland for recommending the Council of Churches to you. It's our pleasure to be of help.

Rudolf Gunther

How like his father, Hand thought, to be working through the Council of Churches when he hadn't much believed in church.

"They showed this letter to the bus driver, and he sent them to Atherton because the address was at the top of the page," said Ms. Fernald, fumbling in her purse. "Now tell your mom I'll be back on the thirteenth. Have her give me a call."

She turned to the refugees. They were climbing out of the backseat, their tawny skin almost purple in the shadows of the pines. Father and son. The man was trim, maybe thirty, some early gray in his temples; the boy was about five and looked both sullen and eager. "Well, good-bye then, I guess," said Ms. Fernald. "Mr. Ziba. All the best. This is Hand Gunther, Rudolf Gunther's son. Hand, this is Nur. Mr. Nur Ziba."

"Good-bye, Miss Athena," said the man, bowing in an old-fashioned way.

Athena? Hand's jaw dropped. What an elegant name for someone so squat and earnest. He watched her jump into her Subaru and roar out onto Route 12. "Good-bye, Aunt Athena," called the skinny little boy, too late for her to hear. He scooped up a pebble and threw it down the driveway.

"You are good to have us," began the father, picking up his suitcase. The boy clutched a Batman lunchbox and held on to his dad's trouser pocket, and began to whine in a language Hand didn't understand.

Nur said, "Your father writes me such courteous letter. Is terrible that he dies so. I am filled with thanks for you. Is many months since we leave our Giti in Tehran. Money is just going until is almost gone. I do not know what to do without you help me so kindly."

They were from Iran, said Nur. Via Belgium and Texas. Slowly they were making their way to Boston, expecting eventually that the absent woman in their lives would arrive from Iran.

His voice was soft. He looked around as he talked. The full summer green of the Berkshires seemed to amaze him. He kept opening his fingers as if imitating the spread of limbs of maple and oak. "In Texas is flat," said Nur.

"In Texas it's flat and in Iran it's mountains but not with trees," said the boy, peering out from behind his father. Hand was surprised the boy's English was so good, and in an American accent, not like his father's.

"Vuffy," said Nur, "this is Mr. Gunther's son."

"Vuffy," said Hand, "is that your name?"

"Vuffy Mohammed Ziba. What's yours?"

"Hand. Hand Gunther."

"What a funny name," said the boy. "Hand. *Hand.*"

"Vuffy," said his father. "Not to make fun of someone's name."

"Hand," said the boy, conversationally, looking at his own hand. "Hi there, Hand. How're you doing, Hand?" He shook his own hand, and giggled in a sweet high voice.

Hand said, "Well, here we are; let me find you a room."

"Baba," said Vuffy, finally having the courage to turn around, "look at this *place!*"

Hand turned to look. The little boy's excitement was so vivid, Hand half expected to see something extraordinary. The motor court, a circle of dirt under some mature beeches, was empty except for Mr. Small's car. Beyond it on the right were the six housekeeping cabins, built in a half circle. Their sills were all rotting into the ground, and pine needles thinly thatched their steep-pitched roofs. Their identical doors fronted on the parking area, and their shades were all drawn—something was wrong with their plumbing, and Rudy had never sorted out what. But they did look nice, Hand figured, with the sun making gold on the roofs and the pine trees crowding in behind and above.

"It's pretty perfect," said Vuffy. "A little house just for me, and one for you, and one for Maman, and one for Uncle Hand!"

"Vuffy," said Nur, "we take up very little space for very short time. Just until we hear that Maman is leaving Tehran, and then we go to Boston to meet her. Remember what we said. You are good boy."

Immediately Vuffy dropped his raised arms to his side and stood, like a little toy soldier, and looked at Hand. With hope and longing, and lips closed.

"The cottages are not ready, the toilets don't flush, no water. We've had the power turned off, too," Hand explained to Nur. "Also they've been closed up and the mildew is awful. The mattresses are like old cake."

"Yes of course," said Nur.

Hand pointed out the motel instead, with the hand-lettered VACANCIES board propped up on the cinder-block wall that hid the garbage cans. "Here's where you'll stay."

"Is very nice." Nur nodded a sideways dip of the head. "Now I think Vuffy should nap. Is still small boy."

"Baba!" said Vuffy, insulted. Hand had seen him from the corner of his eye; he'd wandered off to look at the nearest cabin. He'd been trying out the door. Peering through the window. A spiderweb spooked him and he rubbed his bare arms to get rid of the feel of it.

"Vuffy, you need nap." Hand watched the boy return, reluctantly, to his dad's side, and Hand had to hide a smile. He showed them where Room 3 was, and as the door closed, Vuffy began to whine and wheedle.

Then Hand felt tired himself. Maybe it was the tension of welcoming guests of his father's that had tightened his neck muscles. He went up to his own room intending to read some more of his father's journal. But he couldn't summon the energy. He leafed through some choice back issues of Superman instead. His collection was decent, due to Vida's and his father's regular contributions at birthdays and holidays. He fell asleep with a Classic Comic opened on his bare chest.

When he woke, the boy was standing in the doorway.

"I could help you read if you wanted," he said.

"Oh," grunted Hand, "can you read?"

"I can read the pictures and you can read the words." Without invitation he padded in naked feet across the dusty linoleum floor and climbed

71

solemnly onto the bed. He leaned up against Hand and said, "Which one do you want to read?"

"Which one do *you* want?"

"Which one do you want?"

"Whatever you'd rather, Vuffy. I've read them all before."

"Well," he said, "I think you want this one. Batman. Am I right?"

"Absolutely," said Hand, thinking what a con man this kid was. And he had Hand eating out of the palm of his hand. "How do you know Batman? Do they have Batman in Iran?"

"They have everything in Iran. All superheroes."

"How about in Texas? Superheroes there?"

"Teenage Mutant Ninja Turtles and Batman."

"Hmmm. Do you know who Superman is?"

"You are," he said instantly. "And so is my dad, Baba. And my mom is Wonder Woman."

"And who are you?"

"I'm nobody."

Hand imagined the spirit of Ms. Athena Fernald streaming out of her body—wherever her body was right now, probably on some airplane—and coming to hover over the roof of the Oasis, clasping its hands together and calling out to Hand, a most lukewarm English student, the one poem of Emily Dickinson's he ever admired. *"I'm Nobody! Who are you? / Are you—Nobody—Too? / Then there's a pair of us! / Don't tell! they'd banish us—you know!"*

"You're not nobody, you know," said Hand.

"Read to me, Uncle Hand," ordered Vuffy, changing the subject, snuggling closer, warm as toast. His stiff black hair was like porcupine bristles and poked Hand's chest. Hand stifled a complaint and read two Batmans, a Captain America, a League of Justice, and as dessert *The Story of Ferdinand*. It had been his father's favorite book to read aloud when Hand was little, and Hand still loved it.

"Vuffy?" came Nur's voice, tentatively, up the stairs. Vuffy stiffened.

"Up here, come on up," called Hand. "We're reading."

Nur stood in the doorway, annoyed. "Vuffy. Now. Not to bother our host. Has work to do."

"He's reading and I'm helping him, Baba."

"Vuffy." In a low, quiet voice. Vuffy scrambled off the bed, muttering. Nur apologized. Hand hurried to throw on a T-shirt and said it was okay. When Nur left, Hand sat on the bed and after a while read about Ferdinand again.

◄◄·►►

Over eggs the next day, Nur told Hand the story of their escape from Iran. Nur had been thrown in jail, without formal charges or a chance to appeal. Then he was just as mysteriously released, without warning or explanation. So he and Giti decided the time had come to leave, so their children could be raised safely elsewhere. He had wrapped Vuffy—

73

then just a toddler—in a sleeping roll and set off, penniless and determined, to cross the Iranian desert into Afghanistan. Giti had waited behind because she was six months pregnant and didn't think she could manage the trip.

Nur had hidden by day in ravines and under a brown blanket for camouflage. He hiked by night, following the stars. Helicopters from the border patrols of both countries passed overhead, machine guns poking from the open doors, ready to snipe at deserters. Scorpions by day, artillery by night, and a two-year-old needing to run and play and shout. "Is not good," said Nur.

"I guess not," said Hand. The eggs Nur had made for him were growing cold on the plate. Vuffy was busy with the broom and dustpan. The strangest things amused him.

Then Nur was captured. He was brought to a headquarters in the hills, but the local militia were not all that committed to their task, especially when it came to fellow citizens with small children in tow. With luck, Nur said, he managed to bribe his way out of captivity.

"With what?" said Hand.

"I trade my freedom and Vuffy's for pair of real U.S.A. blue jeans. Sign on pocket says Levi's. More valuable than Iranian carpet to Iranian boy soldier guard."

Hand sat back and laughed. "You traded your jeans for your freedom! And you walked out of Iran in a soldier's uniform!"

Nur wagged a finger. "Not uniform. Just freedom. I go two more nights and two days without trousers. I am naked except for Vuffy and satchel and for one brown blanket."

The rest of the story, Afghanistan to Brussels, Brussels to Dallas, Dallas to Cleveland, and on east toward Boston, Hand heard in bits and pieces. It had been two and a half years now since Nur had left Giti. Giti had abandoned their old home under cover of darkness and gone to stay at her parents' home so she could be available by phone whenever Nur could manage to get through. But Vuffy was growing up without his mother.

It took a little while for Hand to realize that Nur didn't plan to leave the next day. Giti—Nur's wife, Vuffy's mother—wasn't arriving in Boston anytime soon. She was still waiting for a visa to leave Iran. Chances looked good, Nur told Hand; he had smuggled her money for a ticket. He'd worked at a car wash in Texas for a year to save enough money.

Nur showed Hand Giti's picture. It was a snapshot. Giti had what must have been the newborn Vuffy in her arms. She was sitting underneath an apricot tree on a blanket, cross-legged, and smiling up at the camera. She had no veil, which surprised Hand, but Nur said that their kind of Islam didn't require chador. Her hair was a dense black froth. It was pulled back to reveal her face, a heart-shaped ember with a sweet smile.

"Is my whole life," said Nur simply. "My life does not start until she arrives, *inshallah*. Without her I am nothing. I am nobody."

"And the new baby?" said Hand.

"Did not come," said Nur. "Is sick and does not come right." He kissed the photograph and tucked it back into his wallet.

⊰ seven ⊱

Hand called Vida to tell her about the Zibas. A night was one thing, but they didn't show any sign of moving on. Vida said, "Oh well, as long as there's a letter from Daddy, you're okay." But the tone of voice implied she was glad she wasn't involved. "Anyway, you can tell Mom you checked with me first. I can take the heat from here, if there is any." He hung up, grateful for her cleverness. She wasn't a bad sister when she was being normal.

The summer kept throwing situations at him and Hand had to respond, try to act adult. Try to act *all there*. It was harder than it looked.

He woke up the morning after the Fourth of July and clomped down the attic steps to the kitchen. Vuffy was sitting at the counter, trying to spread peanut butter on some bread, pushing and turning a huge sharp kitchen knife. "Baba's still asleep," he said. "Let's play Border Crossing. I'll be the good guy and hide. You be the army guy with the machine guns, and look for me."

"We have a rule here," said Hand. "No playing

guns. It's a policy that my daddy made, and we still follow it."

"Okay, Uncle Hand."

"Vuffy, I'm not your uncle"—Hand stopped when he saw the look of hurt on Vuffy's face—"I mean, not till I have my morning tea," he finished. "I'm just a big old pile of sleep until I get some tea."

"Okay, Uncle Sleep," said Vuffy, and laughed at his invention.

"Uncle Sleepwalker," said Hand, and put his arms out like a zombie, and crashed into the table on purpose. Vuffy roared with laughter, and made him do it again and again.

Vuffy crawled and hung and climbed around Hand like a monkey as Hand did his chores. Vuffy helped Hand collect the green garbage bags in front of the rooms of the Misses Formsby, and Polly Chaucer, and Marvin Small. For once there were some guests, a young couple in Room 9, and Hand changed their towels and brought them some extra soap.

Hand had to stick around all day and staff the office. There was a special event at Tanglewood that night, and it might still be possible to snag some strays. Vuffy dragged a kitchen stool into the office and pulled himself up close as Hand got out the ledger, because this was rent day. Then Hand began to balance the checkbook. Vuffy stapled five envelopes together and wasted two dollars' worth of stamps before Hand caught him. "Vuffy!" said Nur, coming to the door, toweling his hair.

"Don't bother Uncle Hand. Is working. Come here."

"Uncle Hand needs me," said Vuffy. "I can't come here. He needs me to help."

"Don't be silly."

"*Baba*," said Vuffy in an admonishing way. It was almost certain to elicit the Tone of Voice, as Hand was beginning to think of Nur's fatherly rigor. And it did. Vuffy obeyed it, sulking broadly. They went off to work on Farsi, which Hand had learned was the language they spoke in Iran. Vuffy chatted in Farsi pretty well but was still mastering the script. Hand found that the space in the air next to him seemed curiously cold when Vuffy wasn't there.

Polly Chaucer swept in to pay her weekly bill before dashing off to work. "Business is picking up, Hand," she observed brightly. "I see the little family studying at the picnic table in the back."

"Yup." He didn't tell her they weren't paying.

Edith Formsby came in, leaving Frances waiting outside, dangling matching pocketbooks, one for each of them. "We're going for a stroll," said Edith proudly. "We feel the benefits of—"

"The lovely weather," intoned Frances through the screen door.

"A real odyssey—on foot the whole way in—"

"You're as young as you feel—"

"—and the fresh air is a tonic, a regular tonic. Now, young man, our rent—"

"Count it out, Edith, have him count it out in front of—"

"I always do," said Hand, and did. It was correct to the penny, of course. "Isn't that quite a long way to walk? You might get sunstroke."

"We've our *bonnets* on." They had pale, pressed-chicken skin, both of them. They beamed at him from beneath old-fashioned hats with brims as broad as pizza trays.

"Besides," said Edith, departing, "kindly Mr. Small has offered to pick us up at the drugstore at noon. So it's a foot campaign one way only."

It was midmorning before Mr. Small came in with his checkbook. He gave the usual greetings and made the regular small talk. Hand took his check and remarked, "The Misses Formsby said you'll be picking them up in town later on."

"That's right. The stupid old bats," he said. He was sweet as pie to the female sex in their presence, nasty about them behind their backs.

"You on vacation this week?" asked Hand, remembering that Mr. Small's car had been in the lot when Ms. Fernald had dropped off the Ziba family.

"No," he said. "I'm on the night shift now. Pays time and a half, and I really need the money. I've been doing it since Easter, Hand."

Hand made a note in the ledger with his pencil, and then sat there for a few minutes, knocking the pencil against his front teeth, thinking. If Mr. Small had been working nights, he might have been around the afternoon his father had had his heart attack.

He thought of calling after Mr. Small, to know

for sure if he'd been around that afternoon or not. The man might have heard his father call out. Hand wasn't sure what difference it would make if he had. Except maybe Hand's not having called from school to say he'd be late wouldn't have quite the same sting if there'd been someone else around to hear a cry for help.

Hand didn't remember the Stages of Grief that Ms. Fernald had quoted, but suddenly it seemed he'd stumbled into one. Guilt. If he'd *been* there, he might have been able to call an ambulance in time to save his dad. It made him queasy to think about it, but he felt he had to know more about how his dad had died. Then maybe instead of guilt, he could feel grief. Then life could start again, instead of being on hold.

Needing to do something, anything, he closed up the office. He took his old bike and rode to Dr. Pelowski's office. It was closed—long weekend—and he remembered that Dr. Pelowski, who had been his father's new doctor, lived out of town.

A spiffed-up barn on the Upper Falls Road. *Country Gentleman* style; Dr. Pelowski made a specialty of rich summer people's indigestion and nerves, according to local cud chewing. There were low stone walls spiraling out like miniature jetties into the sea of the perfect emerald lawn. On the flagstone terrace the doctor was reading a newspaper. An old Irish setter lolled under the table.

Dr. Pelowski didn't recognize Hand, but he remembered who Hand was when told. The doctor folded the paper carefully so as not to lose his place. He adjusted his hams in the webbed seat and said, "Well then. Master Gunther. I don't usually consult on the weekends. And never at home. You lay siege. My curiosity is aroused."

Hand was so used to adults taking the lead that he hardly knew what he wanted to say. He tried anyway. "Can you tell me what you know about my father's death?"

"You've reviewed the coroner's report?"

"I don't understand enough of it to make sense of it. It just says a heart attack was the cause of death, and some figures and a scribbled conclusion I couldn't read. And how accurately could the time of day be determined?"

The dog shifted, panted a little, and sniffed Hand's sneakers. The man let the opposite fingertips of his hands fall against each other as if by magnetic attraction. The sun was very warm. Only a few circling crows moving.

"I'll give you ten minutes, Master Gunther," said Dr. Pelowski. "You probably don't appreciate the intrusion this visit makes into my R and R time."

Hand wasn't sure what R and R time was, but sat there and nodded.

"A lesson in the heart. Heart as a physical organ. Are you listening, Master Gunther? A heart attack is caused by an acute failure of the pumping action of the heart muscle. Lung congestion occurs. Fluid collects. A person suffering a heart attack may be beset by coughing. Struggle to breathe. Turn blue.

82

There are several causes of heart failure—coronary thrombosis, a blood clot. Or atherosclerosis. In your father's case, I believe, the latter."

"What causes it?"

"One of the lesser coronary arteries had become blocked by fat." To demonstrate, Dr. Pelowski turned his fingers into a ring and tightened the tunnel. "Passage of blood is obstructed. The result is angina. It can cause an acute pain when a person is physically active. Nitroglycerin is a satisfactory treatment of said pain."

"Did Mr. Gunther have blocked arteries?" Hand didn't know why he was calling his father *Mr. Gunther*. Medicine freaked him, maybe.

"Mr. Gunther was prone to problems of that sort. A diet of fried foods, dairy products, the like, would not have helped."

They'd eaten McDonald's burgers and fries four times a week. At least.

"Your father also had a prescription for nitroglycerine," said Dr. Pelowski. "I don't know if he kept the prescription filled."

"What can bring on a heart attack if the conditions are all like that—ready to pop like that?"

"Exertion or excitement may do it. Volatility of any sort. Sexual passion. Terror. Rage. Strenuous frustration. Hard labor. Physical shock. Emotional shock. Tumultuous grief. There are nearly as many ways for the human being to get excited as there are human beings. It's also possible for things to go just like that, with no apparent external cause." He softly snapped his fat fingers; there was no sound.

To the crunch now. "Dr. Pelowski," said Hand, "does a person die instantly with this condition? Say somebody was around and dialed 911. Would that have helped? Could he have been saved?"

"Depends. Every heart is unique," said the doctor, magnificently vague. "Master Gunther, I'd like to remind you that I only saw your father a few times. Yes, he was sometimes depressed. Yet, on the whole, he was even-tempered. He knew about his condition even if you didn't. The surprise of his dying was likely greater for you than it was for him."

He knew he had a heart condition and never told Hand?

"But the real purpose of this visit is not your father, is it? It is yourself."

Hand shrugged, tense and disbelieving.

"You look strong and healthy. Good color. Your heart, though, might be susceptible, too. In time. You will avoid fatty foods and high-cholesterol treats. You will not smoke."

The whole point wasn't Hand. He stood up.

"Sit down. You barged in here uninvited and you will hear me out."

Hand sat down.

"You need to know how your father died, Master Gunther. This I've been trying to tell you. But the pressing question, which says more about yourself than about him, is the one you really want to ask. Not how your father died, but why."

Well, he was right. Why, why? Was it because

Hand wasn't there to dial 911? Or was it because Mr. Small maybe heard a moan, a thud, and didn't bestir himself to go see what was wrong? Was it because Hand's mother had walked out on his father and broken his heart? Was anyone to blame? *Why* did his father die?

"It's the question of adolescence, it is the question of the ages, this *why*," the doctor went on. "The answer is outside our grasp, if there is an answer. Master Gunther, I am not through." But Hand was walking away, disgusted. "There's a colleague I want you to call, a psychotherapist who specializes in teenage separation anxiety and loss issues." It trailed after him, this nosy kindness, completely off the mark.

Hand cycled back, blind to all but his own thoughts. *Was* his father's heart condition a known thing to everyone but him? *Did* his mother know about it?

He would ask her when she got home.

Which was an earlier possibility than he had bargained for. The car was in the lot in front of the motel, and his mother stood, chic and for once totally strung out, a silk shirt partly pulled from her navy skirt, her knuckle pinched between her front teeth. "Good Lord, Hand!" she yelled. "Weren't you to be minding the office during the day?"

"Chill out," said Hand as he jumped off his bike with false calm.

Tranquil was not the term to describe his mother. She lit into him. For closing the office. For ignoring potential trade. Hand stood there staring at her. She was quivering like a bowling pin that's just been clipped—will it fall, will it stand? Her earrings bobbed and spun. He didn't even try to argue.

The Misses Formsby, back from their excursion, came to the door of their room and watched. Mr. Small chose this moment to go to the office to drop an envelope in the outgoing mail pile. Hand couldn't look at any of them. Then, suddenly, Vuffy Ziba came out of the kitchen door carrying an Incredible Hulk comic. He approached them uncertainly, and when his mother faltered at the sight of the five-year-old, he held the colored pages out to Hand and said, "Do you want to read this, Uncle Hand?"

"Uncle *Hand*?" She was dangerously soft of voice. Then Nur appeared at the door and called, "Vuffy. Uncle Hand is busy. Now, come."

His mother exploded. A kind of involuntary recoiling. Hand saw loathing erupt at Nur, though she didn't know who he was or why he was standing in the kitchen doorway. And revealed behind that hatred? Hand could glimpse, just for a second, a terror, an anxiety.

Then her intention reasserted itself. She was marching across the yard toward Nur and Vuffy, her face a war mask of power and anger. Hand sighed. The Iranian refugees were about to join his dad and become ancient history.

Part Three

There is a pain—so utter—
It swallows substance up—
Then covers the Abyss with Trance—
So Memory can step
Around—across—upon it—
As one within a Swoon—
Goes safely—where an open eye—
Would drop Him—Bone by Bone.

⊰ eight ⊱

Hand got another postcard from Uncle Wolfgang, featuring a photo of Emily Dickinson's house in Amherst, and a quote—one line—"Trust in the Unexpected—" "Keep in touch," Uncle Wolfgang wrote again, but Hand didn't. It wasn't a policy decision, it wasn't anything he thought about. It was just that Uncle Wolfgang seemed attached to Hand's family by a hinge that was now missing: Hand's father. Hand didn't know his youngest uncle well enough to know if they'd be friendly or not. He didn't know how to find out, either. Or whether it would be worth it.

So the summer swam on. Weather had no respect for mood, Hand noticed.

The sun shone with its seamless intensity. It flooded the center of the summer with a generous spotlight. The rocky, aromatic Berkshires were swamped with tourists, who did their best to find accommodations other than the Oasis. It was as if they could sense from the road that the motel was the site of a silent standoff, mother and son gripped in a deadlock of resentment. Hand stayed sullen and withdrawn, silently accusing his mom of new complicity in his dad's death: He was sure she must have known about his dad's heart condition. But his intention to ask her had dried up. He didn't care if he ever talked to her again.

For her part, his mother was more and more impatient with her lack of luck in finding a job. With an excess of hostility she threw herself into chores around the motel, loudly exclaiming at least once a day, "From Account Executive to Junior Chamber Maid in one grand, daring move; who would have thought it of me?"

And the Ziba family acted as a sort of international peacekeeping mission.

For to Hand's surprise—yes, the unexpected was to be trusted in, as Emily Dickinson suggested—after the initial blowup his mom reviewed the Zibas' story. She read the letter from Rudy Gunther and sighed. At a crucial moment Vuffy called her Grandma. Far from upsetting her, it made her laugh. "Well, all inherited obligations aren't fiscal," she said. "I don't think by the sound of this letter my husband had actually intended you to live at this motel, Mr. Ziba. But we're not exactly thronged with patrons. I'd rather you just stay here than have to negotiate something else with his friends—all those busybody Good Samaritans." She made a face.

Nur phoned his beloved Giti every couple of weeks. Giti told him that things in Iran were always being held up. The government agency in question was closed for two weeks due to an outbreak of something. Someone was on vacation. Giti needed another signature. She had to go back to Mashad to dig up some documents. It was a new delay with every conversation. But once Hand saw Vuffy's face as he cradled the receiver up against his soft cheek. It looked as if he wanted to suckle from it. He spoke in a quick, smoky Farsi, full of little chuckling twists and tumbles, and he stroked the back of the handset. Nur held him on his lap.

Nur was good with his hands. One day when Hand and his mother came back from a trip to Springfield, where she had had an interview and Hand had shopped for new running shoes, Nur proudly took them to the back of the kitchen. He had dug up four feet of pipe. He had put in a new section and spliced in a valve or a stopcock or something. For an expense of about thirty dollars in hardware, Nur had brought running water back to the six decaying cabins.

"I didn't know it could be fixed," said Hand's mother.

"Neither did Daddy. We thought it was broken for good," said Hand.

"Is nothing broken for good," said Nur. He smiled so hard, Hand imagined his cheeks hurt. Vuffy jigged about, demonstrating the knob, begging them to try it. He led them to the bathroom in the nearest cabin and showed them the toilet. "Look!" he said, and twitched the handle. He turned red with pleasure as the water roared down the toilet bowl.

"Flushed with success, he flushes with success," observed Vida, who came from Bennington every second weekend.

In lieu of rent, Nur spent the summer bringing the cabins back to working order. He cleaned all six of them and replaced the rotten cords in the window sashes. With the windows open the mildewy smell dissipated little by little. He replaced some roofing and built shelves for each bathroom. He even painted the wooden canopies overhanging the doorways a shade of melon paint that he had found on the reduced-for-quick-sale table at the hardware store.

Clare was grateful: Business began to pick up a little. Hand felt encouraged every time he signed in a new guest. The first time a couple *requested* a cabin, the Oasis crew all felt it was a cause for celebration. Nur made supper for them that night. Something called *khoresht*, a kind of dryish stew with chunks of beef. Vida was there that evening, too. She watched him squatting on his haunches, rinsing rice by hand, working off the kitchen floor instead of the counter—the way he used to do it in Iran, he said. "How domestic," said Vida. "Nur, maybe you can fall in love with Mom and she'll never have to cook again."

"He's married," Hand reminded her.

"Khoresht is the best," boasted Vuffy. "Meat and

good stuff. Almost as good as pizza. You're gonna love it, Auntie Vida and Uncle Sleepwalker."

"Spare me," she drawled. "I'm not your auntie. Overtures from a monkey indeed." Vuffy made ape sounds and swung away, happy.

It wasn't long after this that Nur turned his attentions to revamping the canteen. Though there were no proposals to use it, Nur insisted that the canteen shouldn't be allowed to rot into the ground. Hand had steered clear of the place. It had the stink of doom in it. But he was perverse enough to drag himself there and stand in the doorway when Nur launched his campaign. Like feeling a sore, making it hurt, just to know the worst.

So when Nur swept up trash into a pile, Hand helped him with a dustpan. And that's when Hand found the business card with embossed printing. He recognized it instantly. He'd had one handed to him at his father's wake. On the public side it read *Wolfgang Gunther. Theatrical Design Consulting.* His work and home phone numbers and his home address. The only time Uncle Wolfgang had been to visit them at the Oasis was the day after the funeral, and he had divided his time between the cramped living room and Guest Room Number 1, just beyond. So what was that card doing on the floor of the canteen?

On the other side of the business card, in Hand's dad's handwriting, was an area code and a phone number.

Hand excused himself from Nur, and he wandered inside. Puzzling. He found Vida and he got her to come up to his room. He showed her Uncle Wolfgang's card. Was Uncle Wolfgang there when his father died? Why didn't he tell them? Something seemed wrong. Was Uncle Wolfgang hiding something?

"Hand," said Vida, "you are stark raving insane. You know that, don't you?" She settled herself in an old wicker chair and coiled her long, punk-green hair around her forefingers, dragging it out, like moldy taffy pulls on either side of her head. Hand sat on the bed.

"Well, what do you make of it?" he asked.

"Looney *too*-oons," she singsonged. "Smoking in the *show*-ers."

"Vida, cut it out and listen to me."

"Nobody *home* upstairs." She tapped her scalp with a fingernail. "Out to *lu*-unch."

"Maybe Uncle Wolfgang *killed* him," he said, to shock her into talking straight. "They didn't always get along."

Vida's head snapped around. "What do you mean by that?" she said. Her tone was different. He'd gotten somewhere.

"There's both a motive and an opportunity," he said smartly. "Uncle Wolfgang was *up here* in Massachusetts at the time."

"How do you know that?"

"He told me."

"Sheez, are you really in the advanced class at

Atherton? *Big* mistake. What's Uncle Wolfgang's being in Massachusetts got to do with the price of beans?"

"He didn't tell anyone he came *here*," argued Hand. "Just that he was in Amherst earlier that week, visiting the Emily Dickinson house and thinking about death a lot. But he didn't say where he went next."

"I'm impressed, Hand. You've got a great imagination. I'm surprised that furball Fernald thinks you're dull and lifeless in English. But listen." She took hold of the bottom hem of her loose India print blouse and billowed it above her stomach, in and out. "He came to Bennington. He came to see me."

"Oh, right. Sure he did."

"He did. Swear to God. Don't believe me, ask him yourself."

"And you never told me?"

"He was in the area and since we're both interested in the theater arts . . . "

"Just out of the blue? You really think I'm going to believe that?"

"Suit yourself. Push over, will you?" She plopped on her stomach on his bed and began to thumb through the pile of comics. "Wow, Captain America's got bigger tits than I do."

"You're changing the subject."

"Yes I am." She rifled through the stack. At the bottom were some adult comics. "Ah, the good stuff. Hidden away."

"Not hidden away," he said. "I don't like that

stuff as much. It's part of my collection, that's the only reason I keep it." That was the truth, too.

"It makes sense. It's all here in this stack of comic books, Hand." She began to build a case against him. "You bury the more realistic stuff. You like the simpler stories. The ones where the bad guys are the bad guys and the good guys look like Arnold Schwarzenegger. Where right and wrong are cut and dried. You want everybody who has a little quirk to be a villain. Mommy as Cat Woman or Cruella DeVil or the Wicked Witch of the Northeast. You peg her into that, she's got no room to be right."

"That's not true—"

"And now it's Uncle Wolfgang. You don't even *know* him, Hand. What's the point of pinning the badge of Bad Guy on him? So what if he was here? What difference does it make?"

"Daddy would want us to know the truth—"

"Oh *Daddy*," said Vida, as if she was pissed off at him for dying. "Was Daddy really such a good man? The way everybody tells it, he could've walked across the surface of Parker's Pond. Was he so sublime that the only way he could die was as a martyr? Why couldn't he have just kicked the bucket like an ordinary joe? Does it make him too normal? Too likely to have been wrong once or twice in his life?"

"Stop, stop," he cried. "I hate you. *You're* sick. You're just shriveling everything into stupid little pieces. I don't think Daddy was perfect."

In the center of the room, in the light that bled in from the low horizontal windows, there was a vertical trough, a place the shape of a standing man. It was composed by his tired eyes. It was the place where his father wasn't. Hand couldn't picture him there.

"I can't even remember what he looked like, if you really want to know."

"Well, I can," said Vida. "And he was in my opinion a complicated person. Tried to be very good and it didn't always work. You're getting to know Mom again, Hand. She's back in the picture. Can you say in all honesty that she could've been completely wrong and crazy to leave a man so insufferably *right* all the time? Do you see her as absolutely off?"

Though his memory hadn't been able to summon up his father, it had no trouble with his mother. It was almost as if she had come into the room, standing there, waiting for Hand to forgive her. The expectation was unbearable and weird; he shook his head.

"You got to admit, Vida," he said, "it's a rare woman who will walk out on two children. Even if she was miserable with Daddy."

"Haven't you accepted yet that she is her own boss?"

He began to sniff a new hero worship here. "Oh, forget it," he said. "You just hate Daddy. Admit it. You hate him for dying."

"So what if I do?" said Vida calmly. "I can hate

someone and love them at the same time. I'm very talented."

"Get lost," he said.

She stood up and snarled at him like a tiger, and made claws in the air as if to scratch him. *"Rrrrrr,"* she said. "You want to know what I think?"

"No."

"You are locking Mom out so well. *So* well, you don't even see that she's in mourning. Maybe because you don't recognize it in yourself. You should try forgiving her a *little*, Hand. *Pretend* you think she's a human being. She feels very estranged from you."

"I'm not listening," he singsonged. "You're talking to yourself."

"Vuffy's got it right. You *are* Uncle Sleepwalker," she said. She slammed the door when she left. When she headed back to Bennington the next day, she didn't even say good-bye to him. He didn't care.

But as Hand lay awake that night, fanning himself slowly with a Superman, he thought back to the rest of the pages of his father's journal, which he'd finally made himself read.

What lasted—what he remembered—was the sense of mammoth feeling. A sea of sorrow. The thing that his mother didn't demonstrate, at least not to him; the thing that he had no access to either. All this massive longing, this force of heart.

The more familiar his mom was becoming around the Oasis, the more *daily*, the more Hand was determined not to forget the crime she'd committed. Against Vida and him, if not against his dad, too.

It's not grief she feels—she's not capable, he decided. *If she couldn't feel grief about leaving her children, how could she about losing her former husband whom she'd walked out on? What she feels, if anything, is* guilt: *because she knew he had a heart condition and she let him die.* Hand didn't have any proof of this, but his conviction was total.

He couldn't sleep for a long time. He tossed, he turned, he tried to relax. No go. So he flipped through an Incredible Hulk for a while. Then, the night being stubbornly alive, he got up and velvet-footed it down the creaky stairs to the phone. He took Uncle Wolfgang's business card with him and dialed the home phone number in Atlanta. After six rings Uncle Wolfgang answered in a foggy voice. It was two thirty A.M. Hand hung up and went back upstairs and slept. He didn't dream.

✦ nine ✦

The next afternoon, first chance he had, Hand settled Vuffy at the kitchen table—flour-and-water paste, an L. L. Bean catalogue, some blunt scissors, scrap paper. All the tools necessary to keep him occupied. "You stay here and have fun," he said. Then he hurried to the office and told Nur he would spell him for a while. Nur had been staring out the window. "See those rocks at entrance, Hand?" Nur pointed at them. "I paint them white. Move them close, place them in curving line, like this—cars have more time to slow down, look, come in. It will look more like welcome, bring in more business. Also the hedges to clip lower, to see better the sign and the little houses."

"Great idea," said Hand. As soon as Nur left, Hand dialed the number scribbled on the back of Uncle Wolfgang's card.

A bored secretarial voice. "Dr. Chen's line. Who's calling please."

"Uh, uh, Joe Atherton," he said.

"A-T-H-E-R-T-O-N. Number please."

"Uhm—may I speak to the doctor?"

"This is the answering service, sir."

"Oh, I see. Well, if you're an answering service, you can answer some questions?"

She wasn't amused. Hand plowed on. "What kind of doctor is the doctor?"

"Internist specializing in hematology."

"Oh. And that means—?"

"Look. Sir. Leave me your number and Dr. Chen will return your call. I've got other lines to handle here. I can't be yakking all day."

"Well yeah, I know, okay, but just this last thing. Where is this?"

"Doctor's office is East Eighty-fourth Street. Seven fourteen. Top floor. Ring the bell on the left."

"In New York?"

"No, in Chopped Liver, New Jersey. Look, did you *dial* two-one-two or not?"

"I'll call back," said Hand, and slammed the receiver down. He breathed hard and then quickly took the phone off the hook. Irrationally, to prevent her from calling *him* back. Slowly he calmed down. Looked up hematology. The study of blood.

Was Daddy telling Uncle Wolfgang about his heart condition? Giving his doctor's name to Uncle Wolfgang? But why? And in Manhattan? Daddy didn't go to a doctor in Manhattan. Not that Hand ever knew of.

Before he could work it out further, his mother

101

was back from her latest job interview, this one at the Clark Art Institute in Williamstown. Vuffy came running to show her his play made out of the L. L. Bean catalogue models. "This is the Queen and this is the Bad Brother and this is the Baking Cook," he said, pointing. Hand's mother scarcely looked. "Nice, very nice, Vuffy," she said. "Go bother your father."

Hand had slipped the card into his pocket. *Go bother your father.* It was an instruction he remembered from when he was little. Had it been teasing or serious? He felt lanced, nailed to the wall with a tomahawk. A flood of strange sensations rippled through him. How could there be so many basic things he didn't know about the woman who was his mother? Such as if she ever joked or not? The long-forgotten phrase was like a key turning the past back on.

She had stepped out of her good shoes and she padded around in stockings, making up some frozen lemonade. She looked angry in a quiet way. The string of her necklace broke suddenly and the beads rattled to the floor. "Oh, shit," she said, and kicked them away from her. "Hand," she said, as if he'd been stubbornly refusing to help for some time. *"Please."*

"I'll get them—you don't need to bitch at me," he said.

"I'm not bitching at you," she said. "I'm just fed up with interviewing for jobs I'm never going to get. Because the boss's sister is in need of work

102

suddenly. Or because it's an equal opportunity law that you post a job but you already decided on someone in house. I had a perfectly decent position in Seattle. Why it should be so hard to find one here is what I want to know. I'll *never* get this job I interviewed for today, I could see it in his manner. Director of New Acquisitions Funding. And I'd be good at it."

"Why didn't you stay out west?" he said, daring her.

"Ease off, Hand," she said. "I've already been asked that question once today. By a fat slob who had no interest in the answer, and no intention of offering me the job." She poured herself a lemonade. She didn't ask Hand if he wanted one, just stood leaning against the counter with her arms severely folded.

"Well, why *didn't* you stay in Seattle?" he said.

"No comment." Her expression spoke volumes.

"You'd think I deserved an answer at least."

"I came back because I love you," she said, in exactly the same tone with which she'd complain to the grocer that the milk was sour. "I thought it'd be easier for you to stay here. Please behave as if you think me capable of it even if you don't."

He was about to reply, something nasty, when they both heard a high-pitched wail from outside. A thin shriek, then a terrible thud. Hand and his mom ran through the beads, out the door, to where Nur was standing by a tall young tree. "What happened? Where's Vuffy?" Hand yelled at Nur.

A giggle turned their eyes upward. Vuffy was twelve feet above their heads. He had taken a big rock—one of the rocks Nur had been shifting—in his Batman lunchbox up the tree with him, and then launched it off the branch and screamed. "Tricked you, tricked you!" he cried, so excited he was nearly turning somersaults in the tree. "You thought I fell!"

"Get down here!" Nur was furious, and so was Hand's mom. Vuffy almost lost his hold getting down. He started to cry, but he was so tickled with his own cleverness that he kept hiccuping and laughing through his nervous sobs.

His punishment was that he couldn't look at Hand's comics till Sunday. Nur sent him howling to their room. "I hate you. Maman wouldn't care," he wailed. "Maman lets me do everything I want."

Nur apologized to Clare and Hand profusely. "It's not your fault," Hand told him, but Mom said, "You should beware such a gentle attitude with children, Nur. They'll walk all over you as soon as they get the chance."

"Oh, brother," said Hand.

"I'm speaking hypothetically," she retorted, and by now they were both so steamed up at each other that neither of them made supper or came to it. She ate a bowl of potato chips in her room, and Hand took a run into town and got a hot dog and a shake and another hot dog.

He swallowed the watery pink frankfurter in huge gulps, choked on the gluey roll. He was

104

eating fast, out of anger. He should have been able to say to himself: *Someday you won't feel this alone, rejected. Someday the world won't be Mystery Theater. You'll come out on the other side of this and things will settle down.*

The advice that adults kept shoveling his way seemed useless. And his dad—what would his dad have done in all this scratchy family adjusting? The feel of Rudy Gunther, the stain in the air that signified him, his influence—it was fading, little by little, every day. And Hand was going to be left alone with his mother sooner or later, no ghost of his father intercepting them. The idea terrified him.

At the Mall at Factory Mill he ran into Ms. Fernald. She was back from her vacation, tanned and relaxed, turning over the paperbacks on display in the front of the bookshop. "Hand, how're you doing?" she said. "Those people from wherever, have they left?"

"No. They're still here."

"You holding up all right?" She peered at him as if he were a specimen, an alien from another planet.

"I'm just great," he said.

"You got a summer job?"

"Sort of, although I don't get paid. I mean the motel."

"How's business?"

"Picking up," he said.

"Well, Rudy would've been proud to hear that," she said brightly. "He was so depressed with how bad winter business was. I used to say, 'Rudy, this is the Berkshires, this is vacationland U.S.A. Relax, and wait.' But he was awfully anxious."

"I *know* about that," said Hand. He didn't like being told what his father had felt. He also didn't want to say that he suspected Nur's improvements and his mother's financial management might have had a lot to do with things getting better. "Look, I have to go home," he said.

"Want a ride?"

"No," he said. The idea of getting a ride from a teacher horrified him.

"Well, see you in the fall. You're in my Masterworks of the Novel class, aren't you?"

He nodded glumly and wandered home. It was past ten by the time he arrived.

His mother and Nur were both awake, sitting only a few inches apart on the sofa. Vuffy was asleep in Nur's lap, a limp arrangement of limbs and little expressive shudders. The local TV news was bleating into the room. "Hi, Hand, want some ice cream?" said his mom in a fake, everything's-all-right-now voice. *Probably*, thought Hand, *so that Nur could witness how sweet and forgiving she could be.*

"Good night," Hand answered, and went upstairs.

◄◄─►►

The next day Clare and Nur went to a garden

106

center to buy some bulbs for next spring and some perennials and a ground cover. Looking for bargains, they'd pored over a catalogue all through breakfast. Vuffy wanted to go with them, but Mom said, "Oh Hand, he'll be all right with you, won't he? He's so tiresome when we shop—he wants to pick up everything and look at it."

"No I don't," said Vuffy.

"He can stay; I don't care," said Hand. "Doesn't bother me." And it didn't, really. Vuffy sulked for a while, but his usual good spirits came back. He got Hand to play a game of his own devising. He picked up the phone and talked into it, and Hand hid behind the office desk and spoke the part of whomever he was calling.

First Vuffy called Batman, then Santa Claus. "What do you want for Christmas, little boy?" said Hand in a ho-ho-ho voice.

"Bring Maman in your sleigh from Iran," said Vuffy.

When the phone actually rang, Vuffy got it. "YES," he said in a loud, formal voice. "YES . . . YES . . . HELLO TO YOU TOO."

"Vuffy, I'll take it," said Hand.

"WHO? WHO? I DON'T KNOW." Vuffy got suddenly embarrassed and dropped the phone, and it smacked against the metallic desk with a *twong*. Hand drew it up by the cord. "Yes, hello?" said Hand.

It was Mr. Mason from the Clark Art Institute, looking for Ms. Foxworthy. "We'd like to schedule a second interview," he was saying. "We're in a time vise, and need to make a decision quickly. Could you ask her to call back today and confirm a second interview tomorrow morning?"

Hand took the details down on the back of an envelope and hung up. He went hunting for Vuffy, who had taken the keys from their hook and was setting up a play house inside one of the vacant cabins. Hand relented, for once. He would hear the phone from the cabin, or the desk bell in case someone came. So he let Vuffy haul out the comic books and Vuffy's own collection of drawings and figures cut from catalogues, and they played house for the rest of the afternoon, Hand sleepwalking into all the furniture. It convulsed Vuffy every time.

Clare and Nur arrived back with the trunk of the Mazda roped shut around protruding limbs of young trees. "We just went crazy," she said, when Hand came to help carry the greenery out. The root balls in burlap were heavy, and Clare and Nur struggled together with each one. Hand saw Nur reach his arm around his mother's waist at one point, to get a better hold on the tree, he supposed, but it was too intimate for comfort.

His mother didn't seem to mind, however. She was pink with the exertion, and smiling, and talking to Nur in a broken English, making fun of his speech. Hand was mortified, but Nur kept laughing, too, leaning against the car and throwing his head back and howling. Vuffy hopped around doing his monkey routine, scratching his underarms and hooting.

Hand chose not to take part in landscaping design that evening. Instead he read to Vuffy, letting the boy fall asleep in his lap. Then he stared at an old Bette Davis movie on TV, to avoid having to look at his mother and Nur flirting up a storm, right in his presence.

"I don't care where the stupid trees go," he snapped, when Nur asked him for his opinion for the eighth time in a row. "Putting in trees when you know you won't be around to see them grown. I think it's a pretty stupid project myself."

"Well to plant for the future," said Nur. "Not just for yourself, but for somebody else to enjoy."

"Oh leave him be, he's Mister Sulky Adolescent," said his mother. "He has no sense of growth and change. Hand, you're so tight."

"And you're so loose," he said.

"What's that supposed to mean?" she said, but not as if she wanted him to explain, and he didn't explain, he just stomped upstairs.

At the top of the stairs something flickered through his mind, something he was supposed to tell her, but he didn't remember what it was and it served her right anyway.

-<-->-

A few days later she went off again to hunt for work, this time in North Adams. Hand spent the afternoon at the track at Atherton, trying to get in shape for the fall season. They both arrived back at the motel in the early evening. Nur had checked in a couple of guests. Vuffy was building himself a cabin in the middle of the living-room floor with sofa cushions and a blanket.

"How'd it go?" asked Nur, touching her hand softly.

"Same as ever," said Clare. "Overqualified and underemployed, that's me. Hand, how was your day at the gym?"

"Okay," said Hand.

"Oh, look," said Clare, leaning up against Nur, showing him the return address of an envelope she could as easily have read to him. "The Clark Art Institute."

Hand shuddered. "Oh yeah, Mom," he said.

"Shh, wait," she answered, ripping the envelope and unfolding the page inside. She scanned it quickly. *"We regret,"* she read. "Well, surprise surprise."

"I don't know if it's important," said Hand, "but—"

"Since you didn't reply to our request for a second interview—" she read. "What the blazes are they talking about? *—we've been forced to go with our second choice—*"

"I knew there was something I had to tell you, it was the day you bought the trees," said Hand, thinking *Holy moley.* "There was a phone call from Mr. Mason. . . ."

110

Her voice went up a register. "And you didn't *tell* me?" Vuffy came to the door of his invented house and looked out with interest. "I *finally* get a job offer, for something I actually want to do, and you don't even *tell* me?"

"I'm sorry," he said, "it was an accident. I baby-sat that day, remember, and then there was all that work getting the trees out of the car. I wrote it down somewhere; it's probably in the pocket of my cutoffs. I'll go get it—"

"Don't get it *now*, get it four days ago!" She was really screaming. "This is the most hostile, contemptuous, mean-spirited thing you have done, you big, BIG. SELFISH. CHILD."

Nur said, "Clare, is all right, something is to be done, not to be sad," and he put his arms right around her.

"I said I was sorry, I said it was an *accident*," said Hand. "You think I did it on purpose, don't you? You don't understand me at all, and you don't even want to. And I don't want you to, either!"

He stormed away.

"You get back here, I'm not done with you," she yelled.

"Later," said Nur, "is plenty time."

"Back to my own house," said Vuffy loudly to himself, and disappeared beneath blankets and behind cushions.

Upstairs, Hand threw himself on his bed and lay there in the dark. He rolled his arms over his eyes. A sudden summer storm was blowing up, as if triggered by the force of anger downstairs. The wind picked up and pried its fingers under the eaves; he could hear the resistance of the roof beam and the creak of branches, and then the rotating slap of gusts of rain on the shingles. He listened over the sound of the storm to hear if someone was coming upstairs—someone, anyone, even Vuffy—but no one did, and he lay there in the dark, until so much time had passed that everyone must have gone to bed.

He sat up in bed, turned on the bedside lamp, and took out his comics. Such stupid, babyish things. He had wanted to be good, like superheroes, like his father.

He laid out the comics like a quilt on his bed, covering every inch of the surface. Superman, Batman, Wonder Woman, Supergirl, Green Avenger, Spiderman, and friends. The good were all friends with each other. Like Shakespeare and Virginia Woolf and Emily Dickinson, in Ms. Fernald's office. Like Gandhi and Thoreau and Nelson Mandela and Rosa Parks, in his father's pantheon of moral heroes. Hand wasn't included in the cliques of the great and the good.

Not even in his own family. His dad, silent and unresponsive in his grave, under the summer lightning. Mourning the failure of his son to follow in the paths of goodness.

How *would* Daddy have behaved, if he hadn't died? If he'd been put in some coronary care unit somewhere? Would Hand's mother have come back in those circumstances, and if so, what would his dad have done?

He would have forgiven her.

That was what Hand couldn't do, and he knew it.

Hardly thinking, taken over by a swelling sense of sadness, Hand kicked off his clothes and lay down naked in the dark, on top of the comics. He began to cry. He wanted to be held, he wanted someone to hear him, and come. The comics crinkled beneath him as he shuddered into harder tears. He stopped at last, nearly dozing, his thumb dangerously near his mouth as if he were Vuffy's age.

Part Four

Tell all the Truth but tell it slant—
Success in Circuit lies
Too bright for our infirm Delight
The Truth's superb surprise

As lightning to the Children eased
With explanation kind
The Truth must dazzle gradually
Or every man be blind—

Part Four

⤛ ten ⤜

Fall arrived. School began. Tryouts for the track team. A couple of new teachers to break in. Someone named Mr. Secord was taking over Hand's father's class in Conflict Resolution. Ms. Fernald was back, her bouncy best. Mr. Brown announced a Rudolf Gunther Memorial Award for Social Responsibility at the opening middle school assembly. It came as a surprise. No one had bothered to mention it to Hand.

There was noticeably less trace of Rudy Gunther at the Oasis.

Why should that have surprised Hand? Why did leaves turning yellow and red and brown startle him? Why did the smell of mothballed wool pullovers drawn from the hall closet depress him? They were ordinary symptoms of time. It was time for apples in abundance, for bees to blunder into windowpanes in the sunny afternoons, for chrysanthemums to prop themselves up like fake Mexican straw flowers. He knew these things as well as he knew the back of his own hand. So why his jumpiness at life's going on? Was it that his dad no longer seemed as if he were just out of the room, around the corner, off for the day, back in a minute?

Now he seemed to be dissolving.

Hand tried to pump the Misses Formsby for any recollections of strange details of the day that his dad had died. He was hoping to find out where Mr. Small was that day without actually asking him. Hand sat on a bench against the wall in the chilly canteen, the sisters across from him on two cafe chairs Nur had painted peacock blue. Their scented talcum powder puffed off them every time they moved, making Hand sneeze.

"Oh, that wicked, wicked day," said Frances. "That day of darkness."

"It was exceedingly sunny," remarked Edith.

"I spoke emblematically, if I may be allowed to continue—"

"Temperatures in the eighties, I distinctly recall—"

"—well I'm not saying otherwise, but it was indeed a sorry moment for—"

"—the tulips were at their peak though the daffodils had *long gone by!*" snapped Edith. They glowered at each other, sort of affectionately. Frances continued.

"We required a new window fan, so we headed into town. The thought of summer's heat arriving early oppressed us. . . ." "Mr. Gunther drove us to the hardware store . . ." "And he was to pick us up at four thirty. . . ." "We waited—"

"—and considered a cab—" "—but first we called—"

Hand had arrived home from practice at about a quarter to six that afternoon. They would have been dialing just about as he was finishing up in the showers.

"And the gentleman said—"

"What gentleman?" said Hand, surprised

"Why, the gentleman—"

"Someone answered the phone? Someone answered the office phone when you called at four thirty? Who answered the phone?"

"He said—he said—Wrong number. And he hung up." "We tried again—" "—the line was busy—" "the line was very busy. I thought I had dialed wrong." "You probably did, Edith. You often do." "Not five times in a row I don't—" "—I'm not criticizing, naturally. Myself I have trouble with I and E. I before E, etc. Friend and deceive. When I have to write *a friend deceived,* I quail."

Edith was scandalized. "You *never* have to write *a friend deceived!*"

"I *choose* not to." Frances looked smug.

Though Hand worked the Misses Formsby over and over, he could learn nothing more substantial. *Maybe* a man had been here in the motel on the afternoon his father died. Did they think it had been Mr. Small? They most decidedly did not. Mr. Small was a courteous man, and wouldn't have hung up on Edith. Were he to do so, Edith would be surprised and, frankly, disappointed in his behavior. She would feel betrayed. "A friend deceived?" muttered Frances wickedly. They left.

Maybe the Misses Formsby were wrong and it *was* Marvin Small. Or maybe Vida had been lying, to protect Uncle Wolfgang, and *he* was there at the time.

Nur and Vuffy Ziba were still with them. It was beginning to seem to Hand that Giti would never get out of Tehran. Hand's mom said that if they were to stay on, Vuffy had to be enrolled in school. It was the law. She signed some notarized papers swearing that Vuffy lived at the Oasis in Atonquit Falls, Massachusetts, and she accepted responsibility to enforce his school attendance for as long as he lived there. Hand didn't know how she finagled things with Mr. Brown. But off Vuffy went on the lower-school bus to start first grade at snobby Atherton Academy, swinging his Batman lunchbox happily.

Vuffy arrived home at two thirty the first afternoon in tears and fury.

"They hate me!" said Vuffy. "Everybody hates me in that place! They take the thing and they put the thing on it and the other things and they tried to pet me!" His wails submerged his English for a while. Even Clare was tempted from her desk to come see what was the matter.

"What do you mean, Vuffyjan?" asked Nur. "Tell me slow." *Vuffyjan*, Hand had learned, meant Vuffy dear, Vuffy sweetheart.

"They pet me and I don't like it! I *hate* it!" His black eyes glowed.

120

"What means this *pet?*" said Nur, looking at Hand.

"I'm not sure," said Hand. "Vuffy, stop crying and tell Uncle Sleepwalker."

Vuffy didn't usually give in to tears. He was spunkier, more stubborn than that. So this outburst must mean something serious. With a little prying, they managed to find out.

It wasn't just that the children were patting him on the head and trying to ride him like a rocking horse. It was that they were making fun of his un-American name. The first graders couldn't, or didn't want to, get *Vuffy Ziba*. They were calling him Fluffy Zebra.

"Why honey, that's dreadful," said Clare, trying not to smile. "Fluffy Zebra. How insulting. What did you do?"

"I told them my name and told them and *told* them," sobbed Vuffy. "They wouldn't listen."

"How do you tell them? Do you tell them nice?" asked Nur, squatting down to be on Vuffy's level.

"I said, 'My name isn't Fluffy Zebra it's VUFFFFFFFFY ZIBBBBBBBBA!'"

They tried to distract Vuffy, and he stopped crying, but they couldn't convince him it wasn't a catastrophe. Hand made him memorize his first poem: "Sticks and stones will break my bones, but names will never hurt me."

Vuffy went off armed with that the next day, and when he got off the bus in the afternoon he was crying again.

"What happened?" Hand asked him. "Didn't you say your poem to them?"

Vuffy nodded dolefully. "I told them at recess. And then they all picked up sticks and hit me." He had scratches on his legs to prove it.

During study hall the next day Hand got Ms. Fernald's permission to leave the middle school campus and walk down the hill to Atherton Primary. He knocked on the door of Vuffy's classroom. The teacher was a thin, serious woman who poked the air with her elbows, rowing her way across the room from trauma to trauma.

"I have a message for Vuffy," said Hand politely to her. "May I tell him?"

"Yes, Master Gunther. I must say it's very good of your family to take in the Zibas. Quite in your father's footsteps."

"Yes," said Hand. Some family, he thought; some tradition. Without moving from the front of the room, looking out over the pond of little tadpole faces smiling up at him, he said, "Whoever hits Vuffy again is going to get a big fat smack from me. Understand?"

"Master Gunther!"

"Understand, class?" Hand put out a hand waist high to halt the teacher's objections. The students all nodded. Vuffy looked terrified; he was nodding too.

"Now repeat after me: Vuffy Ziba."

"VUF-fee ZEE-bah," they said raggedly.

"That's his name, his only name," said Hand.

The teacher by now was near apoplexy. "We

122

work these things out by a process of negotiation," she whispered hotly. "I've been taking care of this situation, thank you! How *dare* you terrorize them? I will register a demerit."

By lunchtime it was all over school that Hand had threatened to brutalize little kids, making him more distinct from his famous pacifist father than ever.

On the way home Hand walked with Vuffy. They stopped in the cemetery and Hand showed Vuffy where his father was buried. Vuffy didn't seem very interested. It was more fun to jump off the gravestones.

They were about to leave when a kid in Hand's class, Gus Aronian, came scuffling through the leaves with a little girl in tow.

"Say, there's the creep who threatens first graders," said Gus. "Look, Rachel."

"Hi, VUFFY," said Rachel loudly.

"Hi," said Vuffy, shy and grinning.

"Is that your sister?" said Hand to Gus.

"Yeah, is that your monkey?" said Gus.

"This is my nephew," said Hand. But Vuffy started whooping like an ape around the gravestones, scratching himself under his armpits. Rachel laughed, and Gus just shook his head, and said, "Boy, it takes all kinds. Hand, don't go threatening little kids again or I'll punch you in the face."

"I don't expect I'll have to," said Hand. "They seemed to get the message. But isn't your remark a little threatening, too?"

123

"It's just an expression. I had your dad last year for Conflict Resolution," said Gus. "We named our new puppy Passive Resistance."

"Come see him, Vuffy. We call him Pass," said Rachel. She ran on ahead, shrieking and kicking through the leaves.

"Okay, Rachel," called Vuffy. Gus made a face at little-kid friendliness, shrugged, and headed off after his sister.

◄◄--►►

At the end of the third week of September the Gunther relatives appeared out of nowhere. Uncle Emil, Aunt Barbara, Uncle Max, and Aunt Tess. Clare was furious that they hadn't called ahead, just assumed there'd be rooms available.

"Well, the Oasis hasn't exactly been catering to throngs," said Uncle Emil, dismissing her sniffy hesitation.

"We happen to be almost completely booked," replied Clare, which was true. All the work Nur had put into the place was paying off. But there *were* two rooms vacant, so she more or less had to let the relatives stay.

"We didn't invite Hand and Vida down to the Cape as usual this year, and we felt bad about it," said Aunt Tess. "We thought it best not to accentuate the loss of dear Rudy. We've come to say let's let bygones be bygones. What's past is past. You're back with Hand and Vida—I mean

124

you're all back together—and we want to bury the hatchet."

"I never wielded a hatchet," said Clare coldly. "Rather than wield a hatchet I walked out."

"Metaphorically speaking," said Aunt Tess.

The uncles nodded but didn't say a word. Hand sat on the kitchen counter and felt as if he and all the men in the room were brothers, numb, dumb, and cowardly.

"She means," said Aunt Barbara, "for the good of the children. We're not in a position to help except a little, financially. We know Rudy wasn't exactly a whiz at investments and savings."

"I can manage the raising of my own children," said Clare.

"Well, your family has ample resources—" said Aunt Barbara tactlessly.

Clare flared up. "I'm making a going concern of this motel, you know, something that hadn't happened before. But for your interest, my parents cut me off when I married Rudy. And I—when I left here, they would've lavished money on me, but I won't accept their charity. I have some scruples, too. The Gunther clan hasn't cornered that market yet!"

"Don't mind me, Clare," said Aunt Barbara calmly. "I don't mean any insult. Don't take offense."

"Besides," said Uncle Emil suddenly, "nicey-nices aside, there's Wolfgang to think of."

A flurry of glances in Hand's direction. His mom

said, "Hand, you'd better go to the market for some supplies for tonight."

"I want to stay," he protested. "I thought this was about family reunions." But his mother insisted, and off he went.

Later, he tried to pump Aunt Barbara when they were washing dishes. She was unyielding about Uncle Wolfgang. "You tell *me* something," she countered. "This Nur character. Seems to be more than a lodger. Is he from Seattle, too?"

"No, he's a guest from Iran," said Hand, and then caught her meaning. "He's married."

"I see," said Aunt Barbara in a noncommittal tone. "How married?"

"My father invited him, not Mom," he said. "All adults have dirty minds. Nothing's going on, Aunt Barbara. He's a real gentleman."

"He's very handsome."

"You *do* have a dirty mind!" But the very same thought had occurred to him.

"And proud of it," she said. "But I'm just putting the pieces together, Hand. I can't see the whole story all at once, so I keep walking around it and trying things out. Don't mind me. I'm surprised the small-town rumor mill hasn't been working overtime. An attractive man staying as a guest in the home of an attractive single woman."

"She's a widow," he said.

"And widows don't have feelings, I suppose."

He didn't want to answer that, so he said, "*I'm*

still putting the pieces together about Uncle Wolfgang. Come on, Aunt Barbara, tell me."

"Get on with you," she said. "I'll finish up here."

There were two or three other closed-door discussions about something. Hand wondered if he should mention the business card he'd found in the canteen, but something told him to hold it back. He was offended at being left out. Besides, he was busy at work around the motel. Nur and Hand were putting propane heaters in the cabins to winterize them, so they could be rented out during the fast-approaching foliage season. Nur worked hard and constantly worried aloud about Giti. There'd been another massive earthquake in Iran, and he hadn't been able to get through to her for a couple of weeks. Nur was such an obviously devoted husband to Giti, it made his friendly comfort with Hand's mother the harder to understand.

When the relatives left, Hand gave them a cold good-bye. They promised the Cape next year. They collapsed onto Clare with big bear hugs, which she stiffened within. As Uncle Max's station wagon pulled away, Hand read out loud the bumper sticker on the back. *If you can no longer change your mind, how can you be sure you still have one?*

"Busybodies," said his mom, but mildly.

And she didn't give in an iota to Hand's pestering about Uncle Wolfgang. "All in good time," she said, sounding like the Wicked Witch of the West.

A couple of days later Gus Aronian sat down next to Hand at lunch and said, "How's the monkey?" Hand was so relieved to be talked to in the cafeteria that he almost fell into the slang. But something left over from his dad grew up in his thoughts and came out in words.

"You mean Vuffy," he said, not letting Gus get away with calling him a monkey. "He's okay, I guess. At least the kids aren't teasing him anymore."

"The kids like him, according to Rachel."

"Well, I guess it just takes some people time to realize they're liked."

"Yeah, I guess," said Gus.

Hand came home that day walking on air. It wasn't much, but it was a start. He resolved to do better, to make fresh starts everywhere. Starting with his mom. He had figured out that his father would have forgiven her, and so he would, too. He would try, anyway. He found her in the office, trying to load a new spreadsheet program onto Rudy's old workhorse of a personal computer.

"I'd spit at it if I weren't afraid I'd cause a short circuit," she said. "Where's that stupid manual? Why couldn't your father ever file anything where a human being might find it?"

"Mom," said Hand, "when you were young, did you ever want to say something to your parents that you didn't have the courage to say, and then did you regret it?"

"Are you kidding?" said his mother, digging through the bottom file drawer. "If I wanted them to know something, I had to tell the governess. If she thought it of value, she passed it along to my parents and came back to me with their response. Look, here's the catalogue of the computer company; maybe there's a toll-free number I can call." She flipped through it.

"But I mean," said Hand, "suppose there was something really important, and hard to say. Did you just go up to them and—and say it?"

"The less said to my parents the better, I learned pretty early on," said his mom. "They disapproved of almost every word out of my mouth." She tore a page from the catalogue and pulled the telephone on its cord across the desk. "They didn't approve of my sense of humor when I was small, of my mouth when I was a teenager, of my politics when I was grown, or of my husband. I got over the urge to ask them anything." She punched the square keys of the Touch-Tone phone.

"But I mean," said Hand, thinking about how sorry he was he had wrecked her chance for the job at the Clark Art Institute, "maybe sometimes they *wanted* to hear from you?"

"When did my parents ever want to hear from me?" she said. "The answer is never. Oh hello, yes, this is Clare Foxworthy in Massachusetts. I've got a product of yours that makes no sense, and the

129

documentation is unintelligible." Her pen began to scratch cross-hatchings as she listened to the reply. Hand sighed and went to his room. An intention to communicate with his mother, it seemed, wasn't enough. He wasn't getting through.

◄◄--►►

Hand was determined to find out what all the whispering and secrecy about Uncle Wolfgang was about. He lied about having to go to a trial meet, and one Saturday Hand caught the bus to Bennington to talk to Vida. He found her in the library, studying. Dressed in an ugly yellow shirt with black checks about ten sizes too big for her, and purple sweat pants, she looked like a big bumblebee wearing sunglasses. It made him grit his teeth to see her look so artsy and phony.

"Hey guy," she said, as if he showed up every day. That year *Hey* was Bennington for *Hi*.

"Let's go someplace where we can talk," said Hand.

They went to some golden sloping fields nearby, where Vida suddenly dropped to the ground heavily. He thought at first she'd had some sort of stroke or something. Then he realized she was doing some expressive dance therapy routine, contorting and stretching her limbs, working kinks out of her neck, being an annoying showoff. Hand looked politely out to the horizon till she had finished.

"Sit down," she said. "The grass is quite comfy."

"Vida, would you please not ham it up, *please*? I have something serious to talk to you about."

He laid it all out before Vida—repeating the story of his finding Dr. Chen's number in Daddy's handwriting on the back of Uncle Wolfgang's business card, then the Misses Formsby's recollection of a man answering the office phone on the day Daddy died, and the Gunther uncles and aunts visiting their mother out of the blue.

Vida listened, chewing on a straw. "What difference does it make?" she said finally.

Maybe being away from Atonquit Falls made Hand able to say out loud what up till now he hadn't been able to say to himself. "If someone else was around that day, then Daddy's dying all alone wasn't my fault. You know I was supposed to call if I'd be late, and I didn't that day. If only I had—maybe Daddy would be alive today."

Vida slid her eyes toward him without turning her head. "Oh is that it?" she said in a neutral voice. "The blame thing again."

"I don't know about any *again*."

"Well," said Vida, "I simply mean you couldn't *help* blaming yourself when Mom and Dad separated. I couldn't either. All kids do."

"I don't know about that," said Hand. "Maybe, maybe not, but what difference does it make now?"

"It makes a difference," said Vida, with all the power of her freshman Intro to Psych course behind her, "if for the rest of your life you're going to freak out every time something happens that makes you unhappy. If it reminds you, deep down, of how rotten and worthless you felt when you were ten. A recurring pattern," she said, "a pathology: a permanent sickness."

"Thank you Doctor Know-It-All," said Hand. "Now can we get back on the subject of Uncle Wolfgang, which is why I came?"

Vida gave a sigh. "Well, I don't know about Uncle Wolfgang's business card, but I can guess."

"Well, would you please guess in my direction? I've been doing the guessing so far, and maybe I've been out in left field but I don't have a clue."

She lounged. With no particular hurry she began. "The cat's going to be out of the bag sooner rather than later, it looks like. So last spring, Hand? The week Daddy died? You remember?"

"Daddy who?" he said. "Vida, *please*."

"I told you Uncle Wolfgang came to see me? Well, he drove in from Amherst, where he'd been doing that Emily Dickinson research for the play. I was sort of surprised—well, very surprised. But we're getting to be grown-ups and we can make up our own minds about things."

"What do you mean by that?"

"I mean Uncle Max and Uncle Wolfgang don't get along. But that didn't mean I shouldn't see him."

Hand chewed on the inside of his lip. "Don't get along?"

"Why else do you think Uncle Wolfgang never came to the Cape with the rest of us?" she asked. "Earth to Hand. Earth to Hand. Come in, please."

"I thought he just lived too far away. Or something."

"Or something. Exactly. Uncle Wolfgang gives Uncle Max the creeps." Vida gave him a hard, considering look, and continued. "So Uncle Wolfgang arrives. Ta-dah. I was doing props for a production of *Our Town*. So we had a lot to talk about. We went to the Hoosick Arms—a nice place. And Uncle Wolfgang told me something, Hand. He told me he was real sick."

"He who? He himself? Or he Daddy?" But suddenly Hand knew what she was going to say.

"He himself. Uncle Wolfgang told me he's HIV positive—that's the AIDS virus. And that he had already had two bouts of pneumonia and some other infections—and that things didn't look good."

"Why was he telling you? You've never been that close."

"I guess he was kind of practicing," she said. "I don't know why anybody does anything, Hand. He just wanted to. Maybe he was trying to get up the nerve to tell Daddy. I don't know."

"Yes you do," said Hand, sure of himself. "What else did he tell you?"

"That he doesn't have any money," she answered after a long pause. "He's broke and since he's freelance, he has no health insurance. The medicine, whatever it is, AZT I guess, and the

133

doctor's bills and the hospital stay last spring—it cost ten thousand dollars. That Dickinson play was going to be his last job because he was just too tired. The infections were recurring too quickly." Her voice went a little wavery. "He knew that Daddy didn't have much, but he needed money for the medicine. He also knew that Uncle Max and Uncle Emil didn't really have it either. He couldn't ask them. And he wouldn't have asked them anyway, not the way Uncle Max feels about him."

"*You* don't have any money," Hand reminded her.

"But I thought up a plan and followed it through. I got ten thousand dollars."

"*How?*"

"Acting. I had an acting job."

"Vida."

She closed her eyes and opened them again. "A Great Performance sponsored by Mobil Oil. Will not be repeated this season. Two weeks after Daddy's funeral I came back to Bennington and borrowed a friend's car and drove down to the Foxxys' in New York. I told Grandpa and Grandma that Daddy had died in colossal debt, which is partially true, and don't look at me like that—and that Mom couldn't afford to keep me in Bennington, which would also be true if I weren't on full scholarship, but I didn't tell *them* that. And that Mom wouldn't *ever* talk to her parents about money, ever, no matter what the need. And that's *very* true. So I said I was short ten thousand dollars to finish this year and that I could probably get work-study to cover next year. It was my greatest triumph! I was utterly convincing. I drove away with the fattest personal check I ever saw, all their stuffy love for us crammed into a negotiable instrument. Don't *look* at me like that. Because if Uncle Wolfgang needs more money next year, I'll do it again. I *will*." Vida covered her face and primal-screamed into the lapels of her ugly shirt.

"You hardly know him," Hand finally said.

"He's our *uncle* and he's *dying*," she said. "Is that enough reason for you?"

"Well—AIDS is sort of fatal, I know. . . ."

"There's no such thing as *sort of* fatal, Hand. Maybe there'll be a breakthrough this year, next year. A vaccine. A cure. Everybody's working on it. But meanwhile you do what you can. Anyway, I didn't know Uncle Wolfgang saw Daddy. He didn't mention it to me. But he obviously did. And Daddy being Daddy probably knew some New York doctor who had some connections or some new treatments or maybe could get the AZT cheaper. Chen must be an AIDS specialist. And Uncle Wolfgang dropped his card with the phone number and didn't know it. Maybe this was the day before Daddy died, or even that very afternoon—but does that mean Uncle Wolfgang is to blame? Hand, blame isn't the real issue. Nobody's at fault. It's just life's unpredictable pattern, that's all. More to the point, with you, is sorrow; you can't handle it, you can't even recognize it. You plan to keep hammering this into the ground?"

"I can't believe you did that for Uncle Wolfgang," he told her. "You're your father's daughter, Vida. You could win the Rudolf Gunther Memorial Award for Social Responsibility."

"Shut up, Hand. You know what the worst part is? After that sterling performance in the parlor at the Foxxys', I try out for the second year in a row and I *still* don't get into acting workshop. Not even a 'Come back next semester.' So I'm stuck in wardrobe again this year. How pukeful." She stretched an imaginary tape measure from her shoulder out along her left arm.

"But Vida," he had to know, "why didn't Uncle Wolfgang *tell* us he went to see Daddy? Why did he lie?"

"I bet he didn't lie," said Vida. "I bet he just didn't say. Did you actually *ask* him? Maybe he just wasn't ready to have his whole family know—about his illness, not after Daddy's death. You could see it as a sort of kindness. There's only so much sorrow a body can take."

Her tape measure estimated the inches of heart behind his track team windbreaker. "Your heart is only so big. Hearts really can break, you know," she said.

⤙ eleven ⤛

So the mystery of Uncle Wolfgang was solved. But what good had it done Hand? Within a week he would have heard about it anyway. His mother sat Hand and Nur down and told them all about it. Uncle Wolfgang had been in the hospital with pneumonia for most of August. That's why there'd been no Cape vacation that year—the relatives had been tending to Uncle Wolfgang in Atlanta and packing up his apartment.

"I thought they didn't approve of him," said Hand, surprised.

"They don't," said his mom. "Which doesn't mean they're not still his family. Everything's not as cut and dried as you make it out to be, Hand. Anyway, the idea is that he recuperate here. Recuperate or otherwise. Vida approves, but I didn't want to say yes without your both knowing about it."

It didn't come as a surprise to Hand that Nur should now be included in what was essentially a family decision. Hand's mom gave the details of the matter with a breezy matter-of-factness. Hand learned some stuff he hadn't known—or had heard in health class but not really absorbed. She talked about contagion and how rare it is outside of sexual intercourse. "The danger of contamination is minuscule," she said. "Nearly nonexistent to anyone who isn't intimate with a person with AIDS, and I mean intimate in a sexual way. If Uncle Wolfgang should develop any open sores or the like, we'll get in a nurse or reassess the situation then." She sounded as if she were briefing them about a proposal of espionage—detached and slightly harried, her mind on bigger fish to fry back at headquarters.

Nur nodded. Hand had thought that anyone who didn't speak English with a native fluency would be more naive, more easily shocked. Nur never flinched at Clare's definition of Uncle Wolfgang as a man who had no wife but had a male partner whom he dearly loved. "Is family and must be here," Nur declared. "And his friend also."

"Oh I don't think he has one now," said Clare, which ended up being true, Hand found out—he'd died a year earlier. A guy named Bernard.

She turned. "Hand, this may fall hard on you. Uncle Wolfgang is in for a rocky time and so are we. I'd like to say no to this idea; you're having a hard enough time with your father's death as it is." She still spoke about Hand's father as if she'd never met him. "But you can't arrange everyone's lives to suit your own emotional needs."

138

"Oh no?" he said. "I thought you thought otherwise."

"I'm not going to fight you about this. I need to know how you feel about Uncle Wolfgang's living here."

"How do *you* feel?" he asked instead. "I mean you're not exactly best friends with anyone in Daddy's family, Uncle Wolfgang included."

"My feelings don't enter into it. I've made my mind up and that's that."

"Well, then, that's that," he said. "You're the boss. I mean he's got to go somewhere, doesn't he?"

So two weeks later, Uncle Emil and Aunt Barbara drove north with Uncle Wolfgang in the backseat. Hand saw his good looks a different way this time: fatal, stricken, striking. They were reading *The Picture of Dorian Gray* in Ms. Fernald's Masterworks of the Novel class, and Hand was feeling melodramatic. When he looked at Uncle Wolfgang over breakfast, Hand could see the disease in him. He was thinner; he had a persistent cough. There was a constellation of red marks on the skin near his ear, almost like bubbles of peeling paint. The skin was pulled near the corners of his eyes. His hair was still flaxen and shiny, and his expression mainly an internal one.

As far as Hand could see, Uncle Wolfgang didn't really get along with his erstwhile sister-in-law. All his mother seemed to care about was if Uncle Wolfgang had enough to eat, was he warm at night, the new Homer Kelly mystery had come into the library and did he want it? Hand could tell that his mom was being as courteous as she could in a situation she wasn't very pleased about. Hand suspected that Uncle Wolfgang was aware of her mixed feelings about his being there.

Truth to tell, Uncle Wolfgang was a little curt to Hand, too, and Hand was shy around him. Hand remembered the things Uncle Wolfgang had said at Daddy's wake. That he was exhausted. That he'd been thinking about death all week. But it had been his own death he'd been thinking about, not Daddy's. He knew his T-cell count was low, and that the infections were wearing him down. That *The Belle of Amherst* was his last contract with the company. All those Dickinson salvos about death and eternity. The death of his dear Bernard. "I've had other loved ones die, too," he had said.

And Hand had never answered his postcards. They were both aware of that.

Uncle Wolfgang did hit it off with Vuffy, though, after about thirty seconds. Vuffy called him Uncle Wolf. One night after supper Uncle Wolfgang, resting in the kitchen rocker, said, "Please don't call me Uncle Wolf. I don't like that name. It hurts my feelings." He pretended to cry.

"Sticks and stones will break your bones," Vuffy told him seriously, "but names will never hurt you."

"Ah, a poetry lover," said Uncle Wolfgang with a smile. "Defaulting on loans will break my bones—

but never mind. Do you know any other poems?"

Vuffy knew *"Tavalodet Mobarak,"* an Iranian birthday song. But he kept quiet and shook his head. Hand was watching this while trying to do algebra homework. His mom and Nur were sitting in the glaring fluorescent light over the kitchen table, busy sketching out an amateur blueprint for redoing the canteen, laughing at their grand ideas.

"I'll teach you a poem," said Uncle Wolfgang. "It's one of the shortest Emily Dickinson poems I know. It's my motto."

"It's my motto, too," said Vuffy.

"Can't be till you know it. Listen." Uncle Wolfgang was a good reciter of poetry. In crisp phrases, he said,

> Lad of Athens, faithful be
> To Thyself,
> And Mystery—
> All the rest is Perjury—

"What is perjury?" said Vuffy.

"Perjury is lying," said Uncle Wolfgang. "Giving up on the truth."

"As if you can know the truth," muttered Hand, but ducked back into his textbook at Uncle Wolfgang's sharp glance.

Uncle Wolfgang was patient. He said the poem again twice, and explained it. Then he had Vuffy repeat each line, and in two minutes Vuffy wanted to try it all alone. "Listen, Baba," he commanded.

141

"Here I go. No, wait." He twisted his hands together, thinking, then said, "Okay, now. No, wait."

"Vuffy," said Hand, being Ms. Fernald, "focus and centerrrr. Be convincing and surprising. *Now.* Roll 'em."

"Lad of Athens, faithful be—" prompted Uncle Wolfgang.

"Lad of Athens—faithful Bee. Buzzzzzz," buzzed Vuffy. Everybody laughed.

"To Thyself, And Mystery," urged Uncle Wolfgang.

"To Thyself. And Mrs. Bee!" said Vuffy brightly.

Uncle Wolfgang and Hand roared. Vuffy capered. Hand's mom turned red and said shortly, "Don't make fun of a nice poem, Vuffy." Nur just went back to the plans. Vuffy delighted in the fuss he'd caused, and in the next two weeks he memorized Blake's "Tiger, Tiger, Burning Bright" and the poem about Alexander Beetle. He loved poems about animals. He learned part of Emily Dickinson's "I heard a Fly buzz—when I died—" and, getting it mixed up, performed the part of the dying fly with gusto.

◄◄•►►

One afternoon Hand and Vuffy were planting tulips for the spring. Vuffy didn't want to dig, so he plopped the bulbs in their graves, and said the sticks-and-stones poem above each one, and then buzzed like a faithful bee. As they pushed the damp earth back over the bulbs, burying them, they got to talking about things growing, becoming, changing. "What do you want to be when you grow up?" asked Hand.

"I want to be like you," said Vuffy.

"I'm nobody, who're you?" said Hand.

"You're not nobody. You're Uncle Super Hand." Vuffy grinned with a new lopsided toothiness. "A superhero."

"What does it take to be a hero?" asked Hand.

"Uncle Hand," he said, "it takes a long time."

Hand went to put away the trowel and garden gloves. "So do tulips," he said.

Vida's class schedule was easy this semester, so she borrowed a friend's car and came down for a visit for a few days around Halloween. Hand watched the closeness that had developed between her and Uncle Wolfgang, and it gave him pleasure though he felt left out. Vuffy had cottoned onto the idea of Halloween with a vengeance, and Vida, replete with new skills as a seamstress, offered to whip him up a costume. "What do you want to be?" she asked him. "Superman? Batman? A Teenage Mutant Ninja Turtle?"

"No," said Vuffy. "Auntie Vida, can you make me be a fluffy zebra?"

So she bought some cheap synthetic white fur and painted it with black stripes, and stitched and snipped and giggled. Then she took Vuffy off to Albany on the day before Halloween because he was getting overexcited in anticipation of trick-or-treat. There was a dinosaur exhibit at the State Museum there. Hand wanted to go along, but Gus Aronian had asked him to work on an extra-credit science project with him. It was the first time since Hand had moved to Atonquit Falls ten months earlier that he was invited into someone's house. He went, and came home in a good mood around six thirty in the evening. The Mazda was gone.

Hand always had a twinge of—of something, hope, fear, nausea—when he got home and the car was gone. He always thought that someday he'd come home and his mother would have left again. And it would be just like the day he had found his father dead; time would stop, horror would strike, the numbness inside him would protect him from feeling.

He dashed into the office, which was dark. Then he heard a sound in the kitchen and pushed through. His mom was there. Her eyes looked wet and her cheeks streaky. She had on an old flannel shirt of Rudy's. It seemed sloppy and wrong on her.

"Uncle Wolfgang?" asked Hand, alarmed. "What's wrong?"

She looked startled to see him. "In his room if you want him. He's had a bad day." She turned away from him and reached for a paper towel.

"What's the matter with you?"

"Nothing—I'm fine." Her voice was clotted and thick.

"Well, you don't look fine, you look awful."

"How was what's-his-name? Aronian."

"Okay." As if she really wanted to know. "Mom, where's the car?"

"Nur has it."

"*Nur* has it?" Hand was suddenly fed up. "Nur isn't even a citizen, they don't even have cars in Iran, just donkeys. Nur doesn't have an American license. Boy, some people sure know how to use their influence."

"Nur has an international license. Now don't be a spoilsport if you can help it, please." She dug some potatoes out of a sack and tossed them at him. "Make yourself useful and peel these."

"You let Nur go off with the car. Seems to me Aunt Barbara must've been onto something. A little romance here?" Hand was malicious—he knew it, couldn't help it. But he'd been freaked out at the thought of his mom leaving him, even while he still felt so distant from her. The weirdness of it!

But Clare didn't respond to his taunt, at least not directly. She started rinsing lettuce leaves and patting them dry with paper towels. All business and breeding. Foxworthy with a vengeance, Rudy's shirt regardless. "Giti called from Boston," she said with a sigh. "She suddenly got a visa and a flight so fast she didn't have time to call from Tehran or from her stopover in Paris, either. Nur left at noon to pick her up. He couldn't even wait for Vida to get back with Vuffy."

"Well, I hope he crashes," said Hand, senselessly. "It'd serve you right."

"I'm not in the mood for this, Hand."

He plopped the potatoes in the pan of water. "What're you making?"

She slammed a skillet on the stove. *"Khoresht* to welcome Giti. They'll be home in a little while, so I want to have it ready for them. If you're going to help, help. If not, go bother your—go bother your uncle."

"I'll help," he said quietly. "I didn't know you knew how to make *khoresht*," he added, with lethal politeness.

She began to peel onions. "I've watched Nuraddin make it often enough. I think I can manage."

"Nuraddin now is it?"

"That's the formal. Nur is more familiar."

"I see. Nur is rather *intimate*." Hand knew he was being nasty. His mom was upset because Giti had shown up at last to reclaim Nur! Hand could read his mom's emotions in her flat tones, her noisy, broad gestures. He didn't care.

"If you're done with the potatoes—oh, quarter them, not whole, for crying out loud—then cut the fat off this beef and cube it? About half-inch squares. I ought to have had that lazy butcher do it, but I was in too much of a hurry."

Hand began to trim the meat. The knife was sharp—Nur's helpfulness had extended to the kitchen; now they had efficient cutlery. Small streaks of red pushed backward and upward, a greasy film on the flat as he sent the blade in and down.

146

"Here they are!" said his mother suddenly. Then, "No, it's Vida and Vuffy. Don't tell them—Vuffy might get nervous at seeing his Maman again after such a long time. I can't deal with it. Just button your lip."

"Kind of you to consider *his* feelings."

"*Khoresht* again," said Vida, peering at it through outsize mirror shades. "Whatever happened to the knockwurst and bratwurst and sauerkraut we were raised on?"

"We don't eat pork in this house, we're Muslims," said Hand.

"What kind of a bug have you got up your—sleeve?" said Vida. "Mister Personality Plus tonight."

"*Khoresht* is the best," said Vuffy. "Lookit, I'm a dinosaur, Grandma. Lookit." He got on his hands and knees on the linoleum tiles and behaved like a dinosaur in partial paralysis, moving his head jerkily in imitation of the automatons he'd seen. "Lookit, Uncle Sleepwalker, I'm a Muslim dinosaur," said Vuffy. "You be a Christian dinosaur."

"The dinosaurs died out," said Hand ominously.

"You got a cold or what?" said Vida. "Nice shirt, Mom. Come on, Vuffy, let's have a fitting on your zebra costume. I'm not sure if it's fluffy enough." They flounced and roared away.

"Now look," said his mom. "I don't know what kind of mood you're in and I haven't got the patience to drag it out of you. You're going to behave tonight and be polite or I'll—"

147

"Or you'll what?" He pushed the tip of the knife into a chunk of beef and held it aloft. "You'll leave again? Walk out on us again?"

"Hand, just *don't start.*"

"That's what Mrs. Honeybone, the cafeteria lady said." Hand's brain was rocking, bringing things out as through a swinging door, for him to use as weapons. "She said you were going to excuse yourself from this mess of a family again just as soon as you figured out how. She thought that was really great behavior for a mother. I wouldn't recognize what a mother is anymore."

Clare had stopped working with oil and vinegar and cloves of garlic, and she stared at Hand in disbelief. He wagged the knife back and forth.

"Didn't you know Daddy had a heart condition? And didn't you leave him anyway? Compassionate wife and loving mother kills husband by walking out on him. Film at eleven."

His mother rested her fingertips on the counter. "Put that knife down—you'll hurt somebody."

"Pay no attention to that man behind the curtain. Pay no attention to the boy who is saying something to you."

"Put the knife down. This minute."

Hand rested it on the cutting board but kept his right hand tense on the handle. He pushed the beef off the tip so the point was free.

"Now look here Hand," she said to him. "It's not my fault that your father had a bad heart. This nonsense has gone too far. Do you hear me?

148

Besides whatever mess you're making of your memories of your father, you're ruining your chances of getting yourself back on your feet. That should be your main goal these days, and with all this sentimental blame stuff, you're blowing it." She walked across the room and stood five feet from him, hands on hips, chin up defiantly, unblinking.

"If it's not your fault, whose is it?" he asked.

"Nobody's," she said. "It's nobody's fault."

"Nobody's? *Nothing* is nobody's fault! I got home from track practice at five forty-five and he—he was in the canteen, sprawled on the floor—" He couldn't grab his breath. "I should've been on time! I should have called! That was my fault!"

"Calm yourself. Calm down. Hand, give me that knife. Give it here."

Son Kills Mother, Self. Story on Page 4.

"Why did you leave us?" he cried.

"I left because I couldn't stay," she said evenly. "When you're older, you'll understand. I left because your father might have loved me once, but he didn't love me the way I was changing— growing. He couldn't recognize me anymore, I mean not the essential me. And I didn't love him anymore and couldn't stand it. And I left, Hand, to save him as well as myself."

He blinked. His eyes were running and his nose was a mess right down onto his chin.

"If I had stayed. If I had stayed, Hand, I would have made all your lives miserable with my own unhappiness. No, I didn't know his heart was iffy.

149

He didn't tell me. He protected all of us from worrying about him. But *I* knew the strain of fighting me would be bad for him in a psychological way—he who was such a pacifist at heart. And I loved him too much to do that to him. Even as I left him for not loving him enough anymore."

"I don't get it!"

"I loved him and I hated him too. I don't expect you to understand this all at once—or maybe you never will entirely. Don't think you're going to be able to tell the story of your parents' marriage in one summary sentence. Human lives are more complicated than that. And human deaths, too."

He gripped the knife with both hands and bore down on it. Leaning on it, deep into the grain. Through his streaming eyes and choking throat, he had to say two or three times so she could understand him, so she got the message, "But you left *us* too."

She twisted, pinned by the accusation at last. But all she said was "It was my loss. There was no way I could make everyone happy. I'm not your Superwoman. I wasn't going to do you any good being in a loveless marriage, and resenting it every minute of my life. Look, you've split the breadboard."

"It was *our* loss," he argued.

"It *was* our loss," she said. "All of ours." It was the first thing they had agreed on since she had returned. "And Hand," she said softly, "sooner or later you have to forgive me. I'm counting on it."

Hand slumped against the cabinet. His arms and legs felt as if they were going to melt away, leaving nothing but strings of raw nerve. "Okay," he said, not clear what the *okay* was for. "Okay."

"You can't blame yourself, Hand—it wasn't your fault," said his mother, coming over to him but not too close. She sat on the floor next to him and pushed a dish towel toward his face. "It wasn't your fault. I'm your mother, Hand, I know. It wasn't your fault. It wasn't your fault I left. It wasn't your fault he died. *It wasn't your fault.*"

He didn't reach for her or hug her. Nor she him. He just sat there and cried. She twisted the bottoms of her shirt front into a knot and tied them together. She sat waiting for him to calm down. His nasal passages cleared, his eyes felt raw and clean. What did he feel? He didn't know for sure. But if nothing else, he felt awake.

His mom stood up and returned to the salad. Mostly he still hated her. But he got up and rinsed the knife off under the faucet and was just putting it back in the rack when the door opened and Nur came in, leading Giti.

She was a sprig of a woman in a shapeless handknit sweater-coat the color of peanut butter. She had bags under her eyes. Her long hair was lacquered to her scalp by pins and too many days since a shower. The locket of her face, between widow's peak and shy chin almost lost in a grungy gray muffler, was shining like porcelain. She hung

151

behind Nur and clung to his hand and bobbed her head at Hand and at his mom, and slipped off her shoes. "You are—so kind—to us," she said. Her English wasn't as good as Nur's. "Vuffy?" she asked. Her voice was like charcoal crumbling.

"He's off with Vida," said Hand's mom, straightening the shirt collar and pushing her hands through her hair. "I'm so happy to see you." Giti looked as if she didn't understand.

"Baba, look!" came Vuffy's voice, and he burst into the kitchen dressed in a zebra costume, with Vida's feather boa newly stitched down his backbone and twitching off his rump.

"Vuffyjan," said Giti faintly, and then something in Farsi.

And Vuffy, startled, bolted from the room. He was through the passage and across the dark parking lot, and up the tree in a panic.

Hand followed him in a flash, eager for the privacy of the night so his eyes could sting themselves dry. "Vuffy!" called Nur, and Hand heard Giti's astonished gurgle, part a laugh and part a cry. But it was Hand who headed up the pine tree to collect the fluffy zebra and carry him back to his waiting mother.

✦ twelve ✦

After the last meet of the year, a week before Christmas, Hand was startled to find Uncle Wolfgang hunched over the steering wheel, waiting in the school parking lot to meet the team bus. "Your mom is at another job interview at Clark," he said. "Apparently whoever they hired last summer went off one weekend and never came back."

"She shouldn't have asked you to do this!" said Hand. "You shouldn't be out—it's freezing! Think how guilty I'll feel if you go and die on me because of it."

"Right," said Uncle Wolfgang, "you're good at guilt. Well, if I go and die of pneumonia or something, I'm telling you here and now I came to get you because I wanted to. Having a fatal illness doesn't take away my natural human desire to break the rules every once in a while."

They drove out of the parking lot. Hand worried. Uncle Wolfgang was looking pretty skeletal.

"How was the meet?" asked his uncle.

153

"We lost big but I did okay." He had done great, actually: not so much at beating his own personal best, but at fitting in with his teammates. Time had passed, and he wasn't so new to them anymore.

"I never did see the point of team sports," said Uncle Wolfgang. "I always thought football players rushing across the field looked like a pack of animals."

"So does a bunch of ballet dancers rushing across a stage," said Hand.

"Agreed," said Uncle Wolfgang. "If there's anything more senseless than football, it's ballet. But then I always was a loner."

"A lone Wolf," said Hand. He wasn't as uncomfortable with Uncle Wolfgang as he had been.

"Pretty lone," said Uncle Wolfgang. "Even with my good brothers, pretty lone most of the time."

"And with Bernard dying," said Hand. "I can't imagine how hard that must have been for you."

"Sure you can," said Uncle Wolfgang. "Once someone close to you dies, you think about other people dying, and how you'd deal with it. In fact, in a funny way you *have* to imagine it. It's normal. For one thing, thinking about the death of someone you love helps you to appreciate them more while they're alive."

With Uncle Wolfgang's death approaching, Hand felt uneasy having this discussion, yet he didn't have the heart to change the subject. Maybe Uncle Wolfgang needed to talk about it. "What was Bernard like?" he asked. "Would I have liked him?"

"Who can say?" said Uncle Wolfgang. "Turn up the heat, will you?" But the heat was already on full force, baking the front of the car like an oven. "Bernard was a schoolteacher, a verger of his church, and what else? . . . He loved to cook, he loved jazz, he loved to watch tennis on TV. When he died, they wouldn't put the cause of death in his obit."

Hand raised his eyebrows.

"Many people are still scared of AIDS and gay people. You can surely imagine."

Well, Hand could. He nodded.

"How did you get to love him?" asked Hand. "I mean how did you know you loved him, that that's what it was. I don't mean *how*."

But Uncle Wolfgang knew exactly what he meant. "Whoever it is you love," he said, "you recognize it by the habit of loving you learn in your family."

"Oh, great," said Hand. "What habit of loving did I ever learn, with my mother leaving me when I was little and my father dying on me when I was older?"

"Ah, but your mother came back," said Uncle Wolfgang. "Sooner or later you'll realize that's more important than that she left. And your father never stopped loving you. And Vida loves you. And so do I." He grinned as he pulled into the motel parking lot. "Whoever it is, Hand, sooner or later you're going to be in love with someone. And then you'll see how inevitable it is."

One day in January when Hand was shoveling the walks, Marvin Small came over and said, "The Formsby sisters finally remembered to tell me you were asking about the day your father passed away."

"Yeah," said Hand, not pausing.

"They asked if I answered the office phone and hung up on 'em."

"They did, did they?"

"Yup. I told 'em, not me."

Hand turned a corner in the walk and kept on.

"I was here, though; I saw who it was. A lady with mousey brown hair, lots of it. A real tramp."

"Thank you, Mr. Small," said Hand.

"Think nothing of it," he said, and trotted back to his room.

"I won't," said Hand, but he did. The following Monday Hand cornered Ms. Fernald in her office after school.

"Ms. Fernald," said Hand, "were you at the Oasis on the afternoon my father died?"

She looked as if she'd like to light up a cigarette and swish her hair around, but she didn't smoke so she just swished her hair too much. "Yes," she said. "Your father had called me and asked me to come by. He was a little upset. No, he was very upset."

"He called you?"

"We were friends, Hand. Your dad had a genius for friendship. You saw that at his wake. A genius for friendship. Except for with his wife." She sighed and swished. "Her he loved."

Hand nodded. "Why was he upset?"

"The news about his brother. He was there the day before and told your dad about his—predicament."

"His sickness you mean. AIDS."

"That's what I mean. Your dad was grieving for him. He was beside himself with grief. Weeping. So I came over to comfort him." She held her chin up. Behind her, William Shakespeare stared through the glossy finish of the poster at Hand. With her back to the poster, she recited from memory the words that were printed in Ye Olde English Typeface on it, one of her mottos. Hand read it as she spoke it. "'Though justice be thy plea, consider this,'" said William and Athena in unison, "'That, in the course of justice, none of us / Should see salvation: we do pray for mercy; / And that same prayer doth teach us all to render / The deeds of mercy.'"

"I don't get it," said Hand, "the reference."

"I was rendering the deed of mercy as best I could," she explained. "As your dad did and as you will do after him."

For a moment Hand felt they were in a teacher's office with a panel of guest experts: Shakespeare, Gandhi, Dickinson, Thoreau. Everyone looking down—and Rudy Gunther looking down, too—to see how he behaved. Action, Hand, it's action that counts! The invisible heroes, dissolving away like ghosts—but coming back again, coming back when you are most yourself. When you act like yourself.

"Did he die while you were there?"

"No. I left about five; I had to chair the drama club meeting that night. He was just heading for the canteen to do some cleanup work. He must've collapsed sometime in that next hour."

"Did the phone ring?"

She screwed her face up. "Yes. Your dad was in tears, and in no shape to talk to anyone just then, so I answered it; then I hung up and took it off the hook. I couldn't handle it myself."

"The old ladies at the motel were calling; they said a man answered it."

"No, it was me." She began to pack papers into her briefcase. "I'd been crying too, if you must know. My voice must've sounded low." She slammed her briefcase closed, leaving a sheaf of papers like untrimmed piecrust poking out. "I always thought: What if I'd skipped the drama club meeting? I might've been there to help him, to call the ambulance, comfort him."

"Don't say that," said Hand. "You can't blame yourself for something like that." He was at last coming to believe this.

Hand carried Ms. Fernald's stack of textbooks to her car, rendering the deed of mercy as best he could. It was feeble; it was a start.

As he walked home, he thought: What if his mom hadn't left them? Would his dad's health have

158

gotten so poor? Who could say? You could go on forever trying to work it out for sure. Hand thought: *You take what you have, be glad for it. The world keeps turning and the Unexpected can be trusted in; sometimes it's not disaster, but mercy.*

◄◄─►►

The months flew by. Things didn't stay the same. Trust in the Unexpected.

Giti and Nur were beginning to worry that Vuffy was going to grow up entirely as a secular American kid and lose his Iranian and Muslim identity. They had learned that Toronto had a larger Ismaili community than Boston. It was made up of Iranian, Afghani, and East African Indians. In Toronto Vuffy could go to the mosque and be raised in his own traditions. "Is for the best," said Nur to Hand and his mother. "We are so happy here, but we need to have our own home. We have stayed too long here. You have been too kind. After we move, you come to Toronto and see us."

◄◄─►►

AIDS kept drawing the life from Uncle Wolfgang. When Hand came home from school, he fixed the special high-nutrient milkshakes that Uncle Wolfgang needed since losing so much weight. Sometimes Hand read to his uncle.

Sometimes he gossiped about school. Sometimes Hand just sat in the chair and did his homework while his uncle listened to the classical music on WAMC and drifted off to sleep. Now more or less confined to his bed, Uncle Wolfgang lifted his head every afternoon and smiled at his nephew. But the smile looked less and less a function of happiness, and more and more an expression of puzzlement.

One afternoon Uncle Wolfgang motioned to Hand to switch off the radio. "I need to tell you some things," he said. Hand drew his chair close, because it was no longer always easy to tell what Uncle Wolfgang was saying. His uncle looked a little bit like Tweety Pie, big unsurprised eyes in a big head set gently against the pillows, and his neck and shoulders thinned and bony and wasted, hardly able to hold the skull up.

"I go in and out—I can feel it happening," said Uncle Wolfgang. "You know I'm here today, but tomorrow I might not be."

"I know," said Hand.

"Don't be scared of your feelings when it happens, Hand. Be sad, but don't be guilty. Don't be upset. Don't go crazy on yourself."

"Why shouldn't I be upset?" said Hand. "I don't want you to go."

"It's not how long you have," said his uncle, "it's what you make of your time that is important. Years don't mean anything by themselves. Think of a string of pearls, Hand—you can have a string of a hundred beads made out of shoddy, poor-quality stuff. Or you can have a string of thirty-six pearls, each one beautiful, irreplaceable. The necklace isn't necessarily worth more because it's longer. Same with life. It's not the number of years you have in your life that makes it worth something. It's what you do with them."

"Is this supposed to be consoling?" said Hand.

"I need your help," said Uncle Wolfgang. "I've asked to be cremated."

Hand said, "Where do you want the—the ashes?"

"I had a friend," said his uncle, "who had a dog named Candy. She was so upset when Candy died that she had the animal cremated, and she kept the ashes on the piano in a tin labeled CANDY. But guests would always pick it up and try to open it, saying, 'Mmmm, candy,' and she'd have to say, 'Don't, that's Candy, not candy!'"

Hand couldn't believe his uncle was making jokes about his own cremation.

"I don't want a cookie jar labeled 'Wolf,'" he told his nephew. "Hand, I don't want to decide where my ashes go. Maybe when I was feeling stronger I should have thought about it. But Bernard dying, and then Rudy—well, it's been too much. I can't think about it now. Will you figure it out, Hand? Someplace nice. You're up to it? You can handle it?"

"I think so."

Uncle Wolfgang coughed for a few minutes. Hand got him a new box of Kleenex. "Are you okay?" said Hand, when his uncle had caught his breath again.

"Ready to be okay," said his uncle. "How about you, Hand? How are you feeling? Any better at answering that question than you used to be?"

"I'm feeling angry," Hand told him. "I don't want you to die."

Uncle Wolfgang had another coughing fit. Hand looked at the floor until it was over.

"One of these days I'll slip out," said his uncle. "Will you forgive me for that, Hand? If I have a choice, I'd rather go. This is getting hard to do."

"Yes," said Hand, startled to be asked.

"You sound so offended," said his uncle. "I don't think forgiveness is one of your talents. Neither forgiving yourself nor anyone else."

"Don't spend your breath trying to straighten me out," said Hand, a little annoyed, a little embarrassed that his uncle could see the truth.

"When I came to see your father, the day before he died," said Uncle Wolfgang, "he fell to pieces. I never expected he'd take it so hard. Don't you think I have to forgive myself for leaving you without your dad?"

"Don't even talk about it—"

"There's not enough time for all the forgiveness that's needed in life," said his uncle. "Hand, don't blame yourself when I die, and don't blame anyone else."

"*You're* wasting *your* time, and your precious breath," said Hand. "There's nothing to blame for!"

"Ah, but you're good at blame," said Uncle Wolfgang. "Are you ever going to stop blaming your mother for leaving?"

"I have," said Hand.

"Does she know?" asked his uncle. He clutched at his tissue and wiped a knot of phlegm from his lower gum. "Maybe *you* know you've forgiven her, but have you ever let *her* know?"

Hand didn't answer him.

◄◄►►

So it came as no surprise when Uncle Wolfgang died, on a bright Thursday morning in late March. The folks at Irish's Funeral Home kept murmuring, "How tragic! And not even a year since his older brother passed away!" Mr. and Mrs. Brown came, murmuring soft regrets. Ms. Fernald showed up, as full of literary feeling as ever. The Zibas had left for Toronto, but they wired a bouquet of flowers when they heard the news.

Hand thought he would feel numb. But he cried; he cried in a way that felt he would never stop. Once he got started, it seemed that everything tragic in his life welled up and pressed itself forward. And yet, when the tears did stop, there was a sense of being cleansed, being hollow and full of possibility—it seemed strangely as if the life in him were stronger. Hand was astonished. In a good way, he felt older.

But Hand didn't know what to do with the

ashes, which sat on the kitchen counter next to the flour cannister.

◄◄•►►

Before they left Hand and his mom at the Oasis, the Gunthers proposed that in August they should take Uncle Wolfgang's ashes to Cape Cod and sprinkle them in Nantucket Sound. "He'll be included in a family vacation at last," Aunt Barbara said, sniffing.

"Oh please," said Vida. "He wasn't welcome when he was alive, and now you want to drag his ashes along?"

"Vida, don't be rude," said their mother.

"Well, he's not exactly going to be able to send postcards, is he? I don't get it," said Vida.

"What do you think, Hand?" said his mom, and all eyes turned to him.

He knew what he thought, but he didn't want to tell them. Uncle Wolfgang had left the decision up to him.

On the anniversary of his father's death Hand played hookey. In front of the drugstore he caught the eight forty-five morning bus heading east. He had a knapsack with his packed lunch in it, including an especially large bag of corn chips. He also carried the jar of ashes—surprisingly heavy—in a plastic Safeway bag.

Hand was feeling numb and solemn, and not minding it too much. He had his father on his

164

mind and Uncle Wolfgang sort of on the seat next to him. The air was cold for the end of May. A little rain fell, then the sky cleared for a while, though the clouds were an active sort, crossing and recrossing the valleys of the Berkshires, dragging fog and rain behind them. Looking out the bus windows, Hand thought of the two brothers, dead within a year. He was surprised that he missed Vuffy more than he missed Daddy or Uncle Wolfgang. But maybe that was because Vuffy was still alive to miss.

By midday Hand was in Amherst.

He recognized the house from the postcard. Scrubbed red brick with green trim, dignified and seedy in that tilty, askew way that old houses go. It sat on a sharp little rise behind a barrier of stunted cedar hedge. The lawn needed mowing, he was glad to see.

After eating some corn chips, he dumped the rest into the paper bag carrying his lunch. Then he set the plastic sack of ashes and bits into the empty Fritos bag and opened the cannister. He hoped he looked like a high school kid who liked a big lunch.

Although it was noon, there wasn't a procession of wispy, willowy poetesses or bristly academics or much of anybody, really. Hand sat on a granite step at the street end of the walkway and unwrapped his sandwich. Tuna on rye. With his left hand he dug his fingers into the ashes. The stuff felt thin and dry. His hand contorted once, coming upon a harder piece, then gripped again.

He put his hand in the grass then and let it sift out. A very fine hint of it whisked up, like breath in winter air, but mostly it just sat anonymously, disappearing in the grass.

He took a bite of sandwich, let more ashes go. He was very careful not to get his hands mixed up.

Then he got up and strode around the house with the Fritos bag in his hand. Pretended to tie his Reeboks. Good-bye. Admired the stonework in the foundation. Good-bye. Dusted the side lawn with sudden rage and boldness. Good-bye. He couldn't think of a single line of poem. All the holy heroes were quiet.

"Sonny," said a lady at the door, "get off the lawn with your lunch. This is a hallowed literary site, not a picnic ground."

"Sorry," he said, but he wasn't sorry. He was done.

Back on the homebound bus, he ate the remaining corn chips and all the salty crumbs, and licked his fingers on both hands. It rained all the way.

It was dark by the time he got home. His mom was already back from her new part-time job at the museum in Williamstown. She had some chili on the stove. The air was rich with the smell of cumin and hot green peppers and onions; the steam looked almost red when she removed the iron lid to stir things up a bit. The windows were glazed and dripping on the inside. From bulbs that Hand

166

and Vuffy had planted in clay pots just before the Zibas left, two of the first tulips, mixed orange and yellow, bowed in an old clay mustard jar.

She had noticed that the cannister of ashes was gone. "What did you do with them?" she asked.

"I did what Uncle Wolfgang told me to do," he said. "I kept my word."

"You're not going to tell me where you scattered them? You just took it on yourself, just like that?"

"He didn't say anyone needed to know," said Hand. "Can you give me a good reason that it matters?"

"He may have asked you for help, but he didn't ask you to do it alone," said his mom.

"I did what he asked, Mom," said Hand. "I let him go." He was looking at the mail. A letter addressed, in gigantic crooked printing, to Uncle Sleepwalker Hand.

"I hope you have," she said. "I don't want you sleepwalking in grief the way you did all last year. I can't put up with you grappling with another ghost."

Hand thought of Uncle Wolfgang settling in the grass, lifted by the wind. Of the inheritance of ideas his uncle had left behind. Hand thought of his father up in the cemetery, no longer an urgent presence in the gridlock of daily time, but shifting into something more lasting: the past, maybe eternity, even. Hand took in a deep breath. "Mom, you know, Uncle Wolfgang thought that I needed to forgive you, but I told him I had."

"Oh did you?" She sounded a bit sniffy, as if she

thought that Uncle Wolfgang had been something of a busybody to make such a remark.

"And he said I had to make sure you knew it."

"I'm your mother, Hand," said his mother. "Of course I knew it. And you know what? Even if you hadn't forgiven me—it would hardly have made any difference to me. I mean in the amount that I love you. Because I do. You're my son, and you were my son during the years that I didn't live with you. Nothing you could ever do, or feel, would change that. It never did change. It never will."

"Oh," he said. "I guess I wasn't sure."

"Are you sure now?" she asked.

It was an awkward conversation to have, an embarrassing one. But he thought of making the day valuable—a pearl among days—and answered as honestly as he could. "Yeah, I sort of guess I'm kind of sure."

She grinned at that. "About as much assurance as I can hope for. You're not a bad kid, you know that? Hanging on. Trying it out. You're a fighting spirit. Just like your dad was."

"And so are you," he answered back, and escaped this prickly intimacy by heading outside to deliver the mail to the Misses Formsby and Polly Chaucer and Marvin Small.

Hand wiped his forehead with the back of his hand. The stars were spattered against the dark as if they'd just been flung there, as if no one had ever seen them before. He looked at them, thwacking the day's mail into his left palm, and thought: Fighting spirits. All you up there, or wherever you are: reminding us to be alive.

Fighting spirits.

All of you, he thought, and us, too. So are we all.